Love, Lust, and Loyalty in a Girl's Life

Love, Lust, and Loyalty in a Girl's Life

Puneeth J.H.

PARTRIDGE

ISBN: Softcover   978-1-4828-4960-8
             eBook   978-1-4828-4959-2

Print information available on the last page.

To order additional copies of this book, contact
Partridge India
000 800 10062 62
orders.india@partridgepublishing.com

www.partridgepublishing.com/india

We all have a past—some not so great and some not half bad—but one thing to remember: we all have futures.

Samantha T.

Chapter 1

I was enjoying the cool breeze from the window to my left. I turned right, and he turned away! I knew he always looked at me, but he never agreed! I turned towards the board, and could see my chemistry teacher making some jokes which were not funny, but we never had any other option. We had to laugh! Slowly I began to think about things which were not related to chemistry. Pradeep and I were together since last year. We were very caring to each other. I could say we were more than friends, but not committed! He was a typical geek student, but he was very attractive, a bit taller than me and a bit darker than me. He had curly hair. I guess he didn't remember when he last combed his hair! He always found the world's most boring stuff the most interesting ones! I guess I was one of them!

'Smritha, write down!' Poo whispered as my mind seemed far off, in another world. Her name was Pooja Krishnamurthy. I called her Poo. She was one of the most beautiful girls I had ever seen (but not as beautiful as me). Seriously speaking, the only girl whom I trusted from my childhood was Poo. She was very caring. Her skin was as fair as snow, and her lips were as red as blood (with the help of lipstick of course!) Her hair was fine and silky. I loved playing with her hair. The strangest thing about my Poo was that she never spoke to boys! In fact, she never spoke unnecessarily with anyone from my childhood. We studied in the same school together, and hence, we were very close to each other.

She pinched my thigh and signalled me to write down. I started writing down some notes. I hated this subject. 'Something plus something equals something' was what she was teaching! But for me, every chemical equation sounded like 'Smritha plus Pradeep equals love!'

We were all in Class 12. It was called two-year pre-university course in this region. And it was very difficult as the subjects were really dry and not at all applicable to me. We had to attend special coaching classes in early mornings and late evenings along with the regular classes in college. Teacher suddenly raised her voice, 'Class, this is an important turning point of your life! Concentrate.'

I remember hearing this sentence almost every day at least five to six times for the past one month.

For people like me, this sounded like hell. My passion was always music. But due to pressure, I landed up studying here. In fact, the only person who turned my pressure into pleasure was Pradeep.

This time I seriously started writing down some notes, but then I realized that someone was passing by the window. It was Amar. Amar Bharadwaj was his full name. He always stared at me with lustful eyes. He never tried to look away when I stared back. In fact, he looked further inside my eyes. He was a well-built man with great physic and superb fashion sense. He was handsome, with good body language, but looked wild! He was tall and dark and would always have a lustful smile on his face.

Actually, I enjoyed the way he stared at me. He was the one to have ever stimulated the feminine hormones in my brain. But sometimes I hated him. His eyes did not always stare at my eyes! That was the reason I felt uncomfortable with him. I had never noticed Pradeep staring at any other part of my body except my face. That was a pure gentleman. That was why I loved him. But who knows? It is always difficult to judge boys!

The vibration of my mobile woke me up from my thoughts. I always hid my mobile in my salwar's dupatta! I saw the message. It was Pradeep. 'Thinking about me?' It had lots of smileys at the end.

'Who else do I have to think about?' I replied with a blushing emoticon.

I turned at him, and we both exchanged smiles and started to look at our teacher. Poo wrote something on my notes, stared at me once, and continued with her notes. She wrote, 'Stop texting in class, idiot!'

But I continued with the chat, as usual!

'Coffee after class?' Pradeep expected a positive reply.

'Only if it's your treat!' I replied with a smiley.

'Smritha, your salwar is superb! But don't you think that it's too deep at the back cut?' I loved the way he was being possessive of me! Remember, I had told once that it's always difficult to judge boys. No one can say where they are staring at!

Yeah, it's called tie-up long cut! How is it? Isn't it hot?' I purposefully texted like this to irritate him.

'Hot? Never! You'll catch a cold. Cover your back with dupatta!' That's a superb way of texting not to show skin. That's my geek Pradeep! I replied with loads of smiles, 'See you after class, come near the library.'

'Yes, my goddess!' was the immediate reply.

'Want something to eat? I have brought pulav for you!'

'You made it on your own?'

'Come on, you know that I don't know anything about cooking, right?'

'Thank god, I am safe! Bring it near library after class.'

'Hate you.'

'Sorry, goddess! I was joking dear. Won't you forgive your Pradeep?'

I replied with smileys.

The bell rang, and for the next few hours, the class would be handled by the living Hitler. So I didn't even dare to touch my mobile. I met Pradeep at the library after class during lunch break and then promised for coffee in the evening. Poo was with me as usual. In fact, I always took Poo with me whenever I talked with him so that the open secret remained a secret! No one would suspect that Pradeep and I have a special relationship if Poo was with us.

It was lab session in the afternoon, and luckily, my batch was free. Both Pradeep and Poo were struggling with the microscope to see the non-existent vital parts of bacteria, and I was alone sitting near the basketball court, watching Amar playing the game. Seriously speaking, boys looked really hot in sports attire. He had superb biceps and triceps. The sweat was enhancing his contours and shape. He always tried to play a single game so that I would get impressed. I couldn't understand why boys tried to impress me so much; after all, my life was only for Pradeep.

I made it sure that Pradeep didn't notice my attraction towards Amar. Riding my Pleasure, I reached the cafe, which was a bit near to the college. Pleasure was my scooter. It was pink. It was as cute as me. My name was written on the headlight of my Pleasure. In fact, I was emotionally attached to it because it was my mom's last gift to me.

I noticed an autorickshaw stopping outside the cafe, and I could see through the glass that both Poo and Pradeep were in there, sitting at the extreme end points of the seat, maintaining huge gap at the centre! They both got down and came in.

'Are you guys bunking today's classes also?' Poo said looking into my eyes.

'I need not say yes to make you understand.' I smiled.

I could see that the annoyance on Poo's face was melting upon seeing my smile. She gave me a big hug, and then left us.

Chapter 2

Poo's house, 7 p.m.

I was sleeping over at Poo's house that night. We were supposed to study together, but when we both sat together, we did everything other than studies! I looked at my Pinku; it was almost seven. Pinku was my new pink Fastrack watch. I loved it a lot as it perfectly suited my personality. We both went inside Poo's room. I made myself comfortable on the bed. She sat on the study chair.

'Don't you think that you are spoiling your life?' she whispered.

I gave a flat smile. I always thought Pradeep was my future. It wouldn't be spoiled.

'Please, Smritha, why can't you understand? You are not concentrating in class, and you are bunking school in the evening. Are you sure about what you are doing?' She said with a firm voice.

'Have you ever loved anyone?' I said, lying down on her bed.

'What sort of question is that? You know very well that I never loved anyone,' she annoyed.

'Then you won't understand my situation Poo,' I said, watching the ceiling fan, which was rotating slowly.

'You are mad.' She made a disgusting face.

A drop of tear rolled down from my eyes to the pillow. I was still looking up. She came to me and wiped it and kissed my forehead.

'Remembering your mom, Smritha?' she said with a soft voice.

'Poo, it's you and Pradeep who are making me forget my pains. Why can't you understand? I need him in my life.' I kept my words as soft as possible.

'Is your dad normal?' She tried to change the topic.

'He is born abnormal! You can't expect him to be normal.' I was still looking at the fan.

Silence reigned for two minutes. She wanted me to smile, but I didn't want to fake a smile even with Poo. She started studying physics aloud. The intention was to make something to go inside my brain, but I was not hearing much of her physics as I was in my own world.

'Poo, why are we studying?'

'To score well! To get good job and settle down in life.'

'Then?'

'Then what? Live happily!'

'Then?'

'Die someday happily.'

'Why can't I die now? Why should I wait so much?'

My fair cheek turned pink from a hard slap from Poo.

'Look, Smritha, on the day of our death, we should be satisfied with our life.' She held my hand.

'Mom was never satisfied with her life.' I cried, looking at her.

She held my hand more tightly.

I checked my Pinku. It said twenty past twelve. She went to bring dinner. I checked my mobile. Pradeep had texted a few heart-touching messages. I enjoyed the pleasure of what I was feeling and then lay down.

'Smritha, are you all right?' Poo's mom came and sat next to me.

'Little headache, Auntie. Don't worry, by tomorrow I'll be fine,' I said a white lie.

I always tried to see Mom in Poo's mother. Actually, Mom was more caring than this lady, but I was happy at least I had her. Sometime I felt jealous of Poo. She had everything, but I had nothing.

Poo came up with a few chapattis, and Auntie immediately left the place to give us privacy.

'You made these?' I smiled at her.

'Yeah! Nice?' She filled her mouth with chapatti!

I nodded. 'Poo, do you think I should propose to Pradeep?' I expected being scolded.

'Hmm . . . No, Smritha, girls should not propose to boys. It's they who should propose to us.'

'What if he does not?'

'Then he might have never loved you.'

'No, he loves me.'

'Has he told you?'

'No, but . . .'

'That's all, Smritha. You never know boys. Don't expect anything. Just live in the present.'

I had no further question. We finished our dinner, and I started studying seriously. But both of us couldn't study for long. We slept off as we had classes in the early morning at six.

Before I could sleep, I took out my cell phone and forwarded a few heart-touching messages to all the good-looking guys in the class. Poo noticed it and smiled.

'You won't change, stupid.'

'Should I?' I replied with naughty eyes.

'Goodnight.' She smiled and closed her beautiful eyes.

Chapter 3

It was still dark outside. Poo was yelling from the road. I was giving some last touches to my lips with a lip liner, then grabbed my bag and went out. It was shivering cold. She was wearing clothes from top to bottom. I was on my blood-red sleeveless kurti. I saw her trying to start my Pleasure with a kick-start, but she couldn't. I went and gave a kick, and she started! That was my Pleasure. She only obeyed my order!

I was riding, and she sat behind. I checked my Pinku, and she was showing five past forty-seven. We never wanted to go late to school, so I accelerated much more than I normally did and went in full zoom. I just loved the way Poo sat behind, hugging me. She was so warm and made me feel warm. I wish Pradeep would sit like this once!

I zoomed towards the parking lot, getting the attention of guys in our batch. The walking style of Poo was always the same, but surprisingly, my walking style would change whenever I noticed someone observing me. I started walking more consciously, as stylish as possible, towards the class. I managed to sit at the back so that I could message Pradeep. Poo sat at the front bench. I took out my cell phone. No messages or calls from Pradeep. I sent good-morning messages to a few guys and opened my notes.

My class instructor came up, yawning! I guess his wife didn't let him sleep the previous night! He looked a bit exhausted! His name was Mahalingam Prakash. We called him MP. He was in his mid forties, if I was not wrong. He was teaching organic chemistry when a vibration excited me!

'Going organic, dear?' Pradeep texted me with smiles.

'Gooooooood morning, dear! How do you know?' I was shocked that he knew about the class because Pradeep was not in my class and the place where he lived was quite far from here.

'Red top? With ponytail hairstyle?' he again asked me.

I was completely shocked and turned right. I could see his friend pressing something inside his bag! I guess he was texting Pradeep and giving all the information required for a normal 'build up'.

'You have a sixth sense?' I pretended.

'No, but I can feel you. I can see you whenever I close my eyes!' he replied in a style of a typical hero of old Bollywood movies.

'I know the truth,' I replied a bit rudely without any smiles.

'Sorry, dear, I was just teasing. Hope to see you soon. Text you later. Bye,' he ended up.

I didn't even reply just to make him realize that I was a bit angry and expected him to convince me later.

I was not able to control my drowsiness. I guess MP should have conducted sleeping classes instead of organic chemistry. I seriously didn't know which organic rays he sent while teaching. He was simply super talented to make you sleep.

Somehow my Pinku slowly started to move towards seven thirty. In these classes, I always felt she had become slow because of low battery! I went out, controlling my yawn, and was readily waiting to pick up Poo on my Pleasure. I dropped her home and went to mine.

I felt as if I was entering hell. The door was wide open. I could see lots of beer bottles near the sofa and a few porn CDs on the table near the TV. I cursed my dad and went to my room. I always locked my room, so I went in, unlocking the door. I noticed a letter which was pushed into the room between the gap of the door and floor.

Dear Smritha,

> I guess you are sleeping. So I opted to just write this letter so as not to disturb your sleep. I have kept money near the TV drawer. Eat in some good hotel. I might be late tonight. Good day.

He didn't even realize that I was not at home last night. I never wanted his money, but I always took it. This time it was unexpected. I locked the door and went off to the college.

Poo was waiting for me near the parking lot. She placed a tiffin box on the seat while I was putting the centre stand of my Pleasure.

'Your favourite!' She smiled.

'I already had my breakfast,' I lied.

'When will you learn to lie?' She smiled, exercising all her facial muscles.

'You know me well.' I took the box and sat on my Pleasure and started pleasuring my taste buds with some really spicy, hot pulav.

I noticed Amar coming near the parking lot on his new bike. What a style! I always wished Pradeep were as stylish as Amar. But I also knew he would never ever be so, as usual. We both exchanged stares, and he went inside the college, scanning each and every part of my body. My Pinku was warning me to go to class. We obeyed her. No sign of Pradeep.

A vibration was sensed by me in class, and I looked at the message that just arrived at my inbox. I burst into tears! Poo took my cell phone and threw it in my bag. In a few seconds, our teacher noticed me and asked me to go and rest at the girl's restroom. Poo accompanied me.

I was lying down on Poo's lap in the restroom and started crying again. She just consoled me without even saying a word. She checked my message, and she realized what made me this weak.

'You should be strong, Smritha,' she broke the silence.

'I can't,' I cried.

'I understand, dear, but we have to forget the past and live in the present. You are becoming too sensitive nowadays.' Silence reigned.

I slowly went to sleep on her lap. A horrifying scene came in front of my eyes. Water seemed to surround me. I was helpless. I woke up, choking! Pradeep was standing near the door, completely puzzled. Poo went and showed him the message. It said,

> 'Words said by a kid to the waves that took his parents' lives in a tsunami: "No matter how many times you touch my feet, I won't forgive you."'

Pradeep realized the situation. He just walked away, without any reaction. I went to the class the next hour, but my eyes remained wet for many more hours.

Chapter 4

Cyber cafe, 3 p.m.

 I was checking my mails. Poo was on the other system, playing some stupid video game.

'I am lucky enough to finally find you online,' Amar messaged me in a social networking site.

'Isn't this too much? I am not that great.' I pulled back myself from the top.

'You are! You, in fact, don't know how beautiful you are.' I guess he was sincere

'Am I?'

'You are. No second thought about it. Actually, I want to tell you something. Hope you don't mistake me.'

My heart was pounding. I made sure Poo was not noticing my chat.

'No way, anything you want to share is always welcome.' I tried to maintain a polite attitude.

'That red dress looks sexy on you,' he messaged me with blushing emoticons.

I was shocked by the reply. I never expected the fifth word, which was bold.

I immediately deleted all the messages and prepared to sign off.

'Felt bad?' Amar messaged again.

'No, not at all, I was bit busy,' I lied.

'Oh, you are chatting too many at times?'

'No, I'm quite busy. Will message you tomorrow same time, bye!' I replied with smiles.

'Wait, can I have your number?' he was lightning-fast with the reply.

I pretended I didn't see the message, and I signed off from the site and sat blank for a few minutes.

I never let anyone comment on me in such a manner in all these years. I never felt that I should scold him for it. In fact, I was happy with his words. I was confused. I never wanted to cheat on Pradeep. 'But this is not cheating. It was just a casual talk,' I said to myself and went out.

Poo was to ride my Pleasure. I hugged her from behind, and it was drizzling.

'You sure have reduced,' I told her, touching her abdomen.

'Stop it. You act like a lesbian!' she said, shouting aloud, beeping the horn.

'I wish we were!' We both giggled at my answer.

Poo was a slow rider. I let her ride it because it was superb to get drenched in the rain like this. My hair would go very curly when wet, and I just loved that wet look. We almost reached school.

'Ice cream?' I exclaimed.

'You have gone mad!' She was shocked.

'Come on, Poo. It will be fun,' I pleaded.

'I prefer chats,' she said.

'I prefer ice cream,' I said.

And we both ate before going to school. It was chilly inside the class as we were wet, and the fan was spinning at its maximum. I opened my mobile, which was safely placed inside my bag. I had loads of new messages, but I only opened those of Pradeep's. He was concerned and sent me many messages to console me about what happened today. But I wanted to talk about something else.

'What are you doing?' I texted formally.

'Thinking about you!' It was an expected answer.

'As expected! Had coffee?'

'Waiting for company.'

'Who?'

'You.'

'You make me feel shy, idiot.'

'What's there to shy in that?' I realized he was right! Words from Amar didn't use to make me feel shy, but how come I felt so shy now? I wondered.

'Class is starting in a few minutes. Will text you later, bye.'

'Soooooo serious about studies?' he pleaded.

'No, dear, okay, tell me why you were late to the college.'

'Miss you.' He sent an unexpected reply.

'What? You are not answering my question.' I guess he had lost his brain.

'Nothing! I will text you when time comes.'

I knew Pradeep was becoming emotional these days. Actually, this was good news. Every girl loved to see someone special getting attached to her and dropping a tear because he was missing her. I just loved the way he loved me even though he had never told me. I didn't want to reply further. I kept the mobile inside and turned my focus to biology class. My biology teacher was busy making a diagram of the human heart and the circulatory system. He started to explain the accordance of the beating sound of the heart.

At this age, every word about heart sounded superb. In fact, I read a lot about the human heart. And every time I did that, I wondered where the loved one stayed. Arteries? Veins? I didn't know! I turned towards Poo and whispered to her, 'Where does the loved one stay?'

'Cerebellum,' she said confidently, touching her spectacles.

'Oh, the parts near the lower heart?' I replied, seriously looking at her.

She stared back directly into my eyes.

'Cerebellum is in brain!' she said very seriously.

I nodded as if I understood something, and both of us turned towards the board.

'But . . .' I started again.

'Stop, please . . . I will tell you everything after class,' she said sarcastically.

'Attitude.' I turned straight.

The teacher was teaching us about the flow of the blood to the heart.

I was really shocked about the flow of the blood. It was seriously a complicated process. In fact, I was seriously afraid of blood and couldn't imagine huge amount of disgusting blood flowing inside the cute little heart.

Finally, he left the class. Poo was waiting near my Pleasure. My Pinku was ticking eight past twenty. I was still talking to other friends outside the classroom. I noticed her staring at me. There was huge fire in her eyes. I realized the seriousness and dropped her home and went to my house.

It was nine o'clock, reminded my Pinku. I opened the lock. There was no sign of human activities. I realized he had not come yet. I went to kitchen. I could see chicken bones which were threw randomly here and there after eating the flesh. I cleaned it up. I made myself a bowl of noodles and went to my room for a nice sleep.

'Sorry, sweetheart.' I received a text message from Poo.

'Okay,' I replied, expecting more love.

'Look, loved ones do not stay in the heart. The heart is just a vital organ, like the kidneys, lungs, and all. It only helps in pumping blood all through the body,' she explained like my biology teacher.

'Then why did Pradeep say that I stay in his heart?' I blushed.

'It's not like that. In literature, right from the age of Shakespeare, they used the heart as a symbol of love.'

'Why?' I was curious.

'Might be because it's the most important part of the human body.' I guess she was guessing!

'Every part is important,' I argued.

'But the heart is the only organ that works without rest from our birth to death, and even ten minutes after death, I guess. It stands for continuous commitment. So they might say so.'

I was really impressed by the answer, and guess what I did! I asked similar questions to Pradeep and forwarded her message as if I myself thought of it.

Pradeep, Poo, and I were totally tired. He didn't attend classes today as he was exhausted, but Poo didn't allow me to take a rest like that. I badly wanted to rest as tomorrow would be another busy day, but I continued texting Pradeep, and I guess I never realized when I slept!

Chapter 5

Next day, physics class, 11.15 a.m.

'The refractive index is the inherent characteristics of any material. The refractive index of water is greater than that of air. Hence, light travels at a greater speed in air than in water. The refractive index . . .'

My lecturer was yelling. I did not want to hear more of it. All these lessons were already discussed before (I guess). Hence, I didn't want to listen and waste my time again.

My physics teacher was called Fatso. He was so fat that his abdomen belt was hanging tightly as if it were holding tons of weight. He was disgusting. When he started speaking, it was better that the first row students held an umbrella. He spits so much. I wanted his photo—at least to make fun of it after class. An idea flashed into my non-existent brain!

I made a small hole on the sheet of my book and hid my mobile camera in the book such that the camera was at the hole. Somehow I managed to get a photo of a shapeless potato and was just about to take my cell phone back. Poo was observing the whole process and was laughing uncontrollably!

I controlled my laugh by closing my eyes, and I tried to settle myself. Fatso's voice grew louder, but I was not worried as he was still talking about physics. I slowly opened my eyes, and a huge stomach was in front of me. He stopped teaching and was staring at me. Poo sensed trouble and gave her hand some work, writing a few points.

'What's this hole in your book?' He asked with a rude voice. I was shocked. I couldn't speak. Somehow I managed to keep my mobile on my feet and stood up, blinking my eyes.

'I need an explanation,' he again shouted.

'Sir . . .' I started.

'No! Don't even say a word.'

I bent down and hid my mobile with my feet and made sure that Fatso didn't notice it.

'Why are you just standing? What and why were you laughing? Speak out,' he commanded.

This guy was nuts! He asked me to speak, and when I spoke, he asked me to shut up!

'Look, I have seen enough students like you. You are gonna pay for this in the lab.' He sounded even louder.

I couldn't control my laugh as I see Poo overacting, writing the same line again and again just to make others think she was not involved with this. But I controlled myself not to laugh more.

He made me sit with a few warnings. Poo and I laughed about this more than ten minutes after the class. I guess laughter was like virus. If we just heard someone laughing, we got infected and would start to laugh too. Luckily, he didn't ask for my mobile. If he had taken my mobile, almost half of the boys in my class would have received a scolding! I had adult jokes sent by them in my mobile!

Something inside me reminded me to go online. School would start at six, and we had time till then. I went online alone as Poo went home in autorickshaw to freshen up. I had to lie to Pradeep somehow and went online. But the bad news was that he was also in the cyber cafe. I made sure my system was far away from his. I logged in and was happy to see Amar already online!

I signed out very fast, realizing that Pradeep could figure out every move on my profile. I opened up Yahoo! Messenger and wished for Amar to sign in into this as personal chat can be done here. Luckily, he was also there.

'Thank God, I found you here,' I posted my first chat.

'Any problem with Facebook?' he replied.

'No, but let's keep this personal,' I requested.

'No probs . . .'

'I didn't see you in the college today.' I blushed.

'I didn't expect you today. Thanks for going online for me,' he replied.

'What's there in that? I always wanted to chat with you.'

'I wish we were still closer.'

'Nothing is too late,' I replied with more than ten blushing emotions and checked out Pradeep. He was busy laughing and talking over the phone. I made myself comfortable on my seat.

'I didn't see you in the college today,' I said.

'Not well,' he replied.

'What happened? Did you go to the doctor?' I showed some care.

'Fever. To be precise, love fever.' He winked through a smiley.

I knew the topic was turning towards me, so I tried to divert it.

'Do you go to the gym daily?' I inserted some blushing emoticons!

'How do you think I maintain such a body?' He was overconfident.

'I sure agree you have great body.' I started going personal.

I made another quick check on Pradeep. He was still talking over the phone. I felt a bit jealous, hoping it was not a girl!

'Yesterday I asked your number,' he pleaded.

I wondered why boys pleaded for number so much when we can chat on the Net. I didn't get the point why they wanted it. I guess, after all, having my number saved in their mobile might be pride to them!

'I will give it to you next time. Please don't ask reasons.' I smiled.

'Hope you do. Which colour were you on today?'

'Black.' I expected similar compliments as yesterday.

'That reminds me of something. Can I share?'

'Sure.'

'One of my friends proposed to a girl and told her that if she wore black tomorrow, then it meant that she had accepted it.'

'Then what happened tomorrow?'

'She came in pure-white salwar!'

'Your friend felt bad?'

'No! He went to her and said, "I know you loved me from the inside. I realized that when you bent down!"'

He was so bold to post such a message. I laughed at it for a few minutes. Seriously, he sure knew how to flirt with girls. I signed off, saying bye to him, and still noticed Pradeep on the phone. I went near him and started staring at him with anger mixed with curiosity. He noticed my expressions and ended up the call.

'You were on call for the last thirty minutes. Girlfriend?' I said sarcastically.

'Yeah,' he said coolly.

'Kavitha?' I bounced back.

'Nah, her name is Shashikala. She is in Andhra.'

'Childhood love story?' I demanded *no*.

'She is my mother.' I was pacified.

I was so happy to hear that, but still I was curious and took his cell phone and checked. It was only his mom. That was my Pradeep. He never lied to me! I went to school, and he went home after a few minutes.

Chapter 6

Same day, Poo's house, 10 p.m.

'We chatted, Poo,' I told Poo, lying next to her on the bed, sharing the same blanket.

'Who? Pradeep?' She rubbed her nose.

'No! Amar.' I turned towards her.

'Hmmm, the guy from electronics department?'

'Yeah! I met him online.'

'Something something?'

'Nothing nothing! Are you having cold? You are turning pink.' I giggled.

Poo was a very sensitive girl. She turned completely pink when she caught a cold. Her nose and cheeks would be really beautiful to watch at times like this. She sneezed thrice and covered her nose with her handkerchief and whispered, 'Feel like eating ice cream!'

'Are you crazy, Poo? Pinku is indicating we are approaching midnight, and you want ice cream?' I asked with an exclamatory mark on my face.

'You know I'm a strange girl, Smritha.' She smiled, making her cheeks pinker.

'You sure are,' I dragged.

'What are your dreams?' she exclaimed.

'Hmm . . . to get into medical, marry the hottest guy on earth, achieve something in music. Everyone should treat me like a rock star . . . Blah blah blah . . .'

'Whoa, you sure have the worst dreams!' She turned to the other side.

'Worst? Okay, what's yours?' I pulled her back to my side.

'Hmm . . . you shouldn't laugh.'

'I swear I won't.'

'I wish I could go on a long ride all alone on a two-wheeler at midnight!' she said, imagining something on her thoughts.

'What then?' I began to be curious, with mouth wide open.

'I want to build a tree house in the forest and have some time to live with rabbits, deer, and all such cute animals.'

She suddenly sat up and started explaining about this.

'I should be the only human there. There should be lots of flowers in my house, there should be lots of fresh fruits to eat, and there should be one telephone in my house!' Finally she stopped.

'Telephone? To call me up?' I also rose up and sat next to her.

'Noooo . . . to call Corner House, Polar Bear, and MTR for fresh ice-cream home delivery.' She made her statements closing her eyes, and she had seriousness in her voice.

'Then?' I smiled at the stupidity of her dreams.

'Then there should be a small pond nearby. There should be dolphins which should play with me.' She started imaging things.

'Don't want Tarzan?' I started laughing, lying down.

'Look, I told you not to laugh. Get lost.' She lay down, turning to the other side.

She looked really cute whenever she got angry. Her dreams looked imaginary and idiotic, but it showed her innocence. I loved people who were innocent. I loved to stay with them. I guess that was the reason why I started liking Pradeep so much.

'So where am I in your dream?' I asked her sarcastically.

'Nowhere! You laugh at me. That's why I don't tell anyone what I feel,' she said each and every word in great flow.

'How about me cleaning your tree house for you?' I tried to make her smile.

'Don't want! I will do it myself.'

'Poo, I'm seriously sorry. I didn't laugh at your dream. Understand me. You want to make me feel bad and sleep?'

Poo's expression suddenly changed. She smiled at me and came close to me and slept. I found her entire behaviour tonight to be cute. I wish I were so imaginative like her. Hmmm . . . What if I was not! I could always act so! I took out my mobile and texted Pradeep.

'Sleeping without wishing me goodnight?' I wished he was awake.

'You think so? In fact, I was waiting for your message.' It had smileys at the end.

'Can't you message all by yourself? Should it always be me who messages first?'

'How can you think like that, dear?'

'Because you behave so,' I expressed with anger.

'Sorry,' he replied with a sad emoticon.

'Forget it! Guess what? I had a dream now! And you were also in it,' I lied.

'Really? Was it romantic?' I guess he was overexcited.

I started telling him all the dreams of Poo as if they were mine, and I also told him that he was my Tarzan and we lived happily in the forest!

'Shall I tell you something?' he replied in a serious mood.

'Anything! Anytime,' I replied.

'You are really cute. I seriously like you very much. In fact, I have to tell you something, but not now. Let's finish off the public exam first.'

Oh my god, I was on cloud nine. I knew what he meant. I couldn't wait till our exam finished, but still I pretended.

'Tell me now, please?' I requested.

'Please don't force me.' His reply had smileys.

'Shall we sleep now?' I tried to make sure the topics didn't lead to a fight.

'You mean together? You make me feel shy.' He understood my words in a completely wrong sense.

'Idiot, I didn't mean it like that,' I replied with a smiley.

'I know.' There were two winking smileys.

'Goooooood night,' I tried to end up.

'Goodnight, sweetheart,' he obeyed.

Chapter 7

Few days later, ice-cream parlour, 12 p.m.

'You sure look serious about studies,' I told Pradeep.
'I should be, I'm not alone now,' he replied.

'What do you mean by that?' I demanded. I knew what Pradeep actually meant. I was sure he was seriously in love with me. He was hiding it from me, and at the same time, he couldn't control his emotions, so he always tried to express it in indirect ways.

'Nothing! Chocolate brownie is superb with soft vanilla, right?' He started eating.

'You like it very much?'

'Yes I do.'

'More than me?'

Silence reigned for few seconds as Pradeep started to look serious, and he was looking right into my eyes.

'If a person loves someone, then he has to tell that someone as she is his special one.' I made my move.

He remained silent.

'You want to say something?' I wanted him to propose to me.

'Can we talk about this after the exams?'

'What if I will not be alive after the exams?'

'Why do you talk like this, Smritha? You like my eyes getting wet?'

'No, but please, tell me . . .'

'All right! Let me make it clear to you. We both have to do really well in the exams, and we are going to the same college for further studies, okay?' He sounded like irritating. I didn't want to ask him further, but our eyes really spoke much after that. We spent three hours talking almost each and every topic available. He was very much impressed by my messages about my dreams which I had sent him a few days back. He truly believed that the dream was entirely mine, and I was sure he would never get to know the secret behind it.

My Pinku showed almost 7 p.m. I had forgotten my classes also. I checked my cell phone. Poo had called thrice. I texted her that I would pick her after class and came out of that place. It was a bit dark. Pradeep looked at my face with love.

'Don't look at me like that.' I gave a small tap on his shoulders.

'Where should I look then?' He winked.

'Pradeep, we have to spend time till eight thirty.' I smiled.

'We sure can.' He showed me my Pleasure.

'You mean long ride?'

'Yeah.' He looked happy.

'Okay, I will ride.' I started riding my Pleasure slowly. It started drizzling, and I felt so happy. Rain in this situation was too romantic. But Pradeep was sitting too far away from me. Suddenly a light flashed from a car in the opposite direction, and it strained my eyes. When I got my focus right back, there was huge speeding car in front of me, so I applied the brakes suddenly. Pradeep crashed on my back. His cheeks touched my shoulders. A vibration went all over my body.

'All girls are the same,' he said in a low voice.

'What? I didn't understand.'

'They make some handsome guy sit at the back and apply brakes now and then.' He laughed.

I could see his laugh from the mirror of my Pleasure, and I also smiled at his stupid joke.

'Then how many girls have done something like this to you?' I winked at him at the mirror.

He just smiled at my question. We were silent for the next few minutes. We were out of the central city and were on the outskirts. The roads were empty with only street lights here and there. It was still drizzling, and something unexpected happen.

I felt the warmth of his palm over my abdomen. Yes, Pradeep held my bare abdomen, passing his hand inside through the cut of my kurti.

There was some sort of love flowing inside me. I never liked this to happen, but I couldn't stop him. The female hormones inside me got stimulated to its best. I stopped the vehicle and looked at him. He looked hot. The rain had made his hair wet. His thick eyebrows were jet black. Water droplets were dripping from his face. There were three drops of water on his lips. For the first time in my life, I saw lust in Pradeep's eyes. His eyes looked fresh and tender and wanted me to be much closer to him.

'Shall we move on?' he said with double entendre. I didn't say a word. I was shivering. I headed to the road. I saw Pradeep from the mirror moving closer to me. I could sense that his chest was touching my back. My kurti's neck cut was wide. He placed his chin on my bare shoulder. I could hear him breathing near my ears. My heart was pounding. I began to breathe faster. His lips moved from my shoulders over my neck and finally came near my ears.

'You wanted me to tell you something, right?' he asked in a soft voice, which tempted me more.

'Yeeaaahhhh,' I responded, shivering.

'How do you feel when my lips brushed over your skin?'

'Heaven.'

'In fact, I'm in heaven. Your skin is so soft, Smritha. In fact, I always wanted to tell you that I love you.' I heard Pradeep's each and every word with great love.

'Are you serious, Pradeep?' I observed his every move from the mirror.

'Yes, my love. Tell me now, will you love me? Will you marry me?'

'I don't know what to say, Pradeep.'

'Please don't say no, Smritha. I will look after you like a queen. You are my life.'

I wanted to say yes, but I couldn't say anything for few minutes.

'Pradeep, you won't leave my hand in the middle, right?'

'You think I'm that kind of guy?'

'No, Pradeep. I trust you. I did not say anything even when you touched me. Do you think I will let anyone else do this to me? You are special to me. Can't you understand that I have accepted you even before you proposed?'

'Love you.' He kissed me on my ears.

'Love you too,' I whispered, enjoying the kiss.

I checked my Pinku. It was approaching nine in a few minutes. I knew Poo might have reached home by now. I parked in the shade and called Poo. Pradeep, still filled with lust, was sitting on my Pleasure in the rain. She didn't answer my call. I knew she was angry. We both rushed to our respective houses.

'Sorry, sorry . . .' I texted Poo upon reaching home.

'Where were you? At least you home now? Your dad had called me at nine.' She texted me with anger.

'I had pleasure on my Pleasure.' I sent it with loads of smileys.

'What? What do you mean?'

'I'm really happy, Poo. Will tell you everything tomorrow night.'

'I'm really happy to know you are happy, Smritha. I don't even have to know the reason. Just keep smiling like that.'

'Okay! Seriously, I'm missing you.'

'Smiles! Goodnight.'

'Goodnight, sweetheart.'

Pradeep didn't text me that night. I guess he was shy, and I was also feeling shy. So I too didn't text him, and I slept, thinking about his every move today.

Chapter 8

The very next day, 3 p.m.

'Since this morning I have been asking you what happened yesterday. And what is this treat for?' Poo forced a huge golgappa into her small mouth, struggling to eat.

'Can't tell you here.' I was more and more hyped up.

She tried to say something, but she couldn't communicate properly, so I asked her to eat first and then we would talk. We both decided to go on a long walk. I made my first statement.

'I was in heaven, Poo.'

'Then how did you come back?' She giggled.

'Stop it. I'm committed,' I said with pride.

'What? When? How? Who? Where?' She was confused.

'One question at a time, dear.' I kicked an empty tin bottle which was on the road.

'Pradeep, right? How did it happen?'

'Who else can it be? Poo, it was heaven. He proposed to me so softly. He just whispered those three magical words into my ears, sitting behind my Pleasure.' I sounded excited.

'So that's what you meant by pleasure on Pleasure?'

'Yeah, it was too romantic.'

'You have taken this decision seriously, right?' She had become serious.

'Of course, my love.' I smiled at her.

'What about him? Is he serious?' She still sounded unconvinced.

'He sure is. We have not spoken since yesterday. I'm feeling shy, Poo. I guess he is also shy. You know what? Nothing in this world can give this much happiness. Love is superb.' I was shouting at the top of my voice.

Poo didn't look so much convinced, but she was happy to see me happy.

'Smritha, shall I tell something?' She looked really serious.

'You need permission?'

'Look at the situation in your family. You think everything is easy and happens according to what you want?' She sounded with some sense.

'My family is dead. I'm alone.' All my smiles vanished.

'Your dad,' she dragged.

'He is living dead for me.'

'But still . . .'

'Don't you want me to be happy?'

'Forever dear.'

'I will be happy with Pradeep. Please let me be with him, Poo,' I was requesting her, holding her hand.

'Don't worry, Smritha. I will do anything for your happiness.' She smiled.

We both had walked pretty long. We thought of heading back but saw Amar passing by on his bike, giving a stare at me.

'You should stop this.' She winked.

'Poo, he is the one who stared at me. I'm always loyal to Pradeep.' I smiled.

'How about Pradeep?'

'Hmmm . . . I hope so. In fact, I have doubt about Kavitha. I have noticed her talking to him every now and then.' I sounded a bit jealous.

'Oh my god, it has started. Just yesterday you were both committed, and today you started doubting?'

'Hmmm, after all possessiveness is part of love.' I smiled.

'No, it makes lovers torn apart.' She sounded meaningful.

'Poo, next week is his birthday. I should make sure it will be his best birthday.' I sounded excited.

'And this week there is a unit test, don't forget that.' She tried to irritate me.

'Poo, tell me, where shall we . . . ?'

'What do you mean by that? So soon you guys want to do that?' She giggled.

'I mean . . . where shall we celebrate?' This time I made myself clear.

'Hmmm . . . Celebration should be meaningful. Let's go to an orphanage.' I liked the idea.

Chapter 9

Same day, 11 p.m.

'How long will you not talk to me?' I texted Pradeep. 'I can't live long without talking to you,' he replied back very fast.

'Shall I tell you something?'

'Anytime. Anything.'

'Miss you.' I really was missing him.

'What we are doing is correct, right?'

He was a scaredy-cat.

'Yes, dear, nothing wrong. If love is wrong, that means nothing in this world is correct, and everyone should have been a prisoner.'

'You won't leave me, right?'

'Not even in my dreams.'

'I'm still scared.'

'Pradeep, remember, we only have one lifetime and only one life to love.'

'I trust you, dear. Please don't let me go'.'

'No, dear, I promise.'

Pradeep seemed scared of commitments. In fact, this was the first time I got committed in a relationship, but I guess I was more comfortable than him.

'We should study well, dear. We should prove that even people in love can score well in exams.'

'Yeah, Pradeep! We will, sweetheart. In fact, if we study well, it's better for our future.'

'Am I privileged to hear the sweetest voice on earth now?' he sounded sweet.

'Shall I call?' I knew he wanted me to.

'Then why do you think I'm asking you?' He requested me to call.

'Wait, two minutes. I will check out Dad and come back.'

I always wanted Pradeep's voice to be heard at this time. I wondered how his voice would sound when he spoke low at this time.

'Hellooooo . . . Is this my princess?' He sure knew the art of making me feel special. I started laughing.

'I'm speaking to you. Say something.' I could not control my giggling. I said nothing but kept laughing.

'If you keep laughing like this at midnight, then you may scare the people around you.' He made me laugh even more. Finally, I stopped laughing and turned serious.

'All the people I see around are you.' I made a strong statement.

'Hmmm . . . Then go and hug anyone, thinking it's me!' He laughed, making a stupid statement.

'Idiot, monkey, stop it. Then what are you doing?'

'Dreaming.'

'Dreaming? About what?'

'Talking to my dream girl this late at night, is it not a dream come true?'

'You make me feel special.'

'Because you are special.'

'How come the geek talks about life so romantically? Attending any classes for this course?' I started laughing.

'Yeah, you are my teacher.'

'And what about the fee?'

'How much do you want?'

How much can you give?'

'All my love!'

'Don't you think you are paying something which is priceless?'

'You deserve it, my princess!'

I loved the way Pradeep loved me. He, in fact, made my heart beat fast. His every thought brought me intense happiness, and I seriously wanted this happiness to remain with me forever. I wanted to talk about the plan I made with Poo. I wanted to tell him to celebrate his birthday with me. I moved on with my conversation. 'Sooo . . . what is my prince planning for next week?' I started.

'Next week? What's there to plan?' he pretended.

'Sweetheart, I know your birthday is next week. Come on tell me. What's the plan? Am I in it?'

'Hmmm . . . You really want to be part of it?' He tried to irritate me.

'Obviously, will you tell me or not?'

'All right, dear, in fact, I have not planned yet. I want to spend the whole day with you. Can I? Will you be with me, please . . .' He sounded serious.

'Why are you pleading me so much? It's not just your wish. I wish the same. I will take you to a special place. Don't ask me about it now. It's a surprise.' I sounded interesting to him.

'What's that? Taj Mahal?' He laughed.

'Stop joking. You sure will like the place. I will call Poo also. Is this all right with you?'

'Nooo, please, I want to be alone with you. I won't be free when she is around.'

'All right, we both are going together.' I smiled.

'On your vehicle, right?' Both of us started laughing, remembering about that night.

'Of course! But maintaining some distance,' I pretend to be decent.

We both continued our chat on and on, and when we noticed the time, it was two o'clock in the morning. Pinku was warning me to sleep. I promised to speak with him like this every night and slept with a warm feeling in my heart. It was the feel which made you feel like in heaven.

Chapter 10

Two days later, 5 a.m.

I was struggling on my bed, feeling completely uncomfortable. I rose up from bed. It was still dark and spooky. I walked towards the door in the dark and opened the door. The opening of the door lock was very loud. I could hear the rain. Suddenly there was a flash of light near the window. I guess it was lightning. I went to the kitchen and drank water. I was thinking what woke me up. It was Amar. I saw him in my dream. He was too close to me. He was on top of me, on my bed. He was sleeping over me, holding my hands tight, and I couldn't move. He was kissing me on my upper chest. I didn't like the feeling but still could not stop him. He was too seductive. I guess I was also enjoying the romance. It took fifteen minutes for me to come to reality and to realize that it was just a dream! I began to think about Amar. True, he was hot. But why was my mind getting towards him? After all, I was committed to Pradeep. But having secret fantasies like this was not wrong. Everyone dreamt of someone or another person on their bed. It was a universal truth—except few specimens like Poo. And even having such person as a casual friend was not wrong after all. Then why was I avoiding him online? Why didn't I give him my number? Was I in love with him? Was I hiding my emotions towards him to myself and cheating myself? Was I scared that I would start loving him when we both came closer? I didn't know. Sometimes I do not understand myself!

What would Pradeep do if he came to know about this fantasy? Would he respect it? No way! No one would accept things like this. I couldn't stand it whenever he spoke with Kavitha, even though they were just friends who rarely spoke. Then how could I expect Pradeep to accept my sexual attraction towards another guy? It was impossible.

What if I maintained our friendship and kept my fantasies secretly? After all, no one would come to know about this. Only I knew it, and no one would obviously comment or doubt on friendship. But what if I got involved sexually with him when we got closer? It would be like two-timing. I didn't want to cheat on Pradeep. He was my life. But still I was attracted to Amar. I didn't know what was happening to me! Was I flirting? Wasn't my love to Pradeep true? My love towards Pradeep was 100 per cent pure, and I definitely didn't want to lose him. I couldn't live without him. I took out my mobile, and I checked my Pinku. It was showing five past thirty minutes.

'Goooooooooooood morning, dear.' It was Pradeep's sweet message. It felt as if he was whispering in my ears while I was reading the text message.

'Sorry,' I replied spontaneously.

'For what? Are you all right, sweetheart?' His innocence made me feel guilty.

I replied with a blank message.

'What happened? Please tell me, dear. You need not say sorry. I trust you. I know you won't do any mistakes.'

He had sent smileys at the end. But smile didn't come on my face. I was feeling guilty, thinking that I was cheating on Pradeep. I thought of going online today evening and tell Amar that I was committed. I would explain my situation and would finally come out of all this today itself.

'Reply, dear. Don't scare me up,' he replied after my silence.

'I am sorry for not texting you first,' I lied.

'Don't feel like that at all, dear.'

'That happens because I always think about you. Every day I wake up, and the first thing I remember is you.' He brought tears to my eyes for the priceless love.

'Love you, Pradeep,' I told him from the heart.

'Love you too, dear. No school?' He reminded me about the daily activities of my life. I texted bye to him and made myself ready for school. I went around the whole house, but no sign of dad. I guess he was never home the whole night. Who knew with whom he was sleeping with!

I switched on the TV for a quick review of news. But accidently, I switched on the DVD player. A porn movie started playing. I started cursing Dad for bringing all these porn videos at home when he had such a big girl living with him as his daughter!

I went to switch off the DVD player but couldn't. The video looked uncontrollably lusty. I had never watched any of these things even though Dad had them at home. But this time, I couldn't control myself. I went and checked the lock of the door and played the video from the beginning.

I started feeling pleasure all over my body. I started realizing the pleasure points in my body. Without my knowledge, my hands started moving over them. I began to imagine myself in the video. The guy in the video was Amar. I was losing myself.

A vibration in my pocket made me to view the new message. It was Pradeep asking me whether I reached school safely. I felt uncontrollably guilty. I switched off the TV and sat under the cold shower!

'I'm bad,' I told myself.

'I'm proving to be the daughter of my dad,' I shouted aloud.

The cold water droplets were slashing on my face. It was like the water was taking away all my sins which I had committed this morning. My guilt feeling started to reduce with time. My hate and anger towards me were flowing along with the water. 'The sins are gone now,' I told to myself. My clothes were wet. I took my bath later on and left for the college, thinking what reason I could give to Pradeep and Poo for my absence in morning class.

Chapter 11

Day before Pradeep's birthday, 9.45 p.m.

I was lost in his words. His sweet voice penetrated right into my heart through my ears. He was talking unstoppably. Both my ears were pleasured with the earphones, which helped me hear him. I was talking to him over the phone for the past half an hour. Actually, he was the only one talking.

'Hello, say something! You slept or what?' he yelled at me.

'Hmmmm . . .' I just hummed.

'Are you sleeping or standing or sitting and talking to me?' he asked.

'Floating!' I blushed.

'You make me smile sometimes.'

'You make me smile always.'

He started to tell about his plan tomorrow. He wanted to spend his entire day with me, but only I knew where he would be.

'Today you are not going to receive any calls till one o'clock. I want to talk to you. I want to wish you a happy birthday first,' I commanded.

'I guess Kavitha might call at twelve. Hmmm, can I talk to her for a few minutes?' He was trying to make me go mad.

'Will kill you . . . and even that girl. I guess she has done some black magic on you. She will never be spared,' I started scolding Kavitha without my knowledge.

'Stop it! I was kidding . . . Man, you take things so seriously. All right, tell me one thing. How can I even talk to anyone else other than you? Smritha, I love you. I don't even care whoever might call. I won't bother. I only want the greetings from the love of my life, my lucky charm.' He took away my anger in a few minutes.

'I know what my Pradeep is. I was just checking out how much you love me.' I smiled.

'Hmmm . . . Came to know about it?'

'No, I guess I will never know about it.'

'Oh really? Why?'

'My love, every time I try to measure your love, I find it higher than what I have measured before. The more I measure it, the deeper I discover. I guess I would keep on discovering the never-ending love. I wish I die discovering it.'

There was silence for a few minutes. Both of us didn't say anything. I guess Pradeep loved my words. Unknowingly, there were tears in my eyes. I didn't know how he discovered my tears.

'I wish I could wipe those tears and kiss them.'

'How did you know that my eyes are wet?'

'Because mine are wet.'

'Love you, Pradeep . . . Love you.'

'Now why are you making things so emotional? Stop it. Can I see my life smiling?' He made me smile.

I was checking out my Pinku. It was already eleven thirty. I wanted to surprise him with something, so I made all the arrangements. I searched for the sheet in which I wrote a special note for him.

'What are you doing? What's all that sound?' Pradeep noticed my work as I didn't speak much.

'Nothing, I'm just searching something . . . All right, now tell me, what gift do you want tomorrow?'

'You!'

'I'm already yours, Pradeep. Come on, ask something which you can keep for long.'

'I will ask when the time comes.'

'When will that time come?'

'I wish it comes soon. Now shall I hang up the phone?'

'Why?' my voice roared like a lion.

'I am getting a lot of calls. Many calls are waiting.'

'Are you trying to irritate me? Try cutting the line, you will face the consequences,' I told him in anger.

'No, my love, I just teased. Now wish me a happy birthday, I'm waiting.'

'Wait, I have set my Pinku to the exact time. Let her show twelve. Five more minutes left.'

'Hmmm . . . all right, I will wait.'

'Pradeep, lie down.'

'Yeah . . . I have been lying down for long time.'

'Good, close your eyes.'

'All right.'

'I know, my love. This might be funny to you, but still it's done with love. Please accept it. Don't speak anything, just listen.' My voice softened, and I began to sing him my own song.

As I lie in my bed every night,

The moon shines through my window right . . .

Its bright light gives me company.

While you are so far away,

I pretend it's you to make me feel safe.

As I start to fall asleep,

I'm woken by the thoughts of your face.

And finally, when I do drift away,

I never want to wake up.

I want to stay with you in my dreams . . .

When I do wake up,

I glance to see if it was just a dream or if you were actually there.

I always wake up in an empty bed,

But emptiness will not always be in my heart as you will fill in it, my love.

Love you. Happy birthday.

I sung the entire song as romantically as possible using all my musical talent. I could hear Pradeep crying.

'This is the best birthday gift I ever had.'

'Liked it?'

'Loved it, but it's not fair to make me cry on my birthday.' He was trying to tell me that he cried with happiness, thinking that I didn't notice his tears, but I pretended.

'Did I sing so badly?'

'Idiot . . . Love you.' I could imagine his face, saying these words. In my imagination, he was the happiest man on earth. I could see tears in his eyes and cheeks, but he was smiling. It was a wonderful night.

'Happy birthday.'

'How many times will you greet me?'

'Keep counting . . .'

We kept on talking for long . . . We both showed love to each other. I kept on greeting him every now and then. He kept on counting them. Pinku was warning me that she was ticking away and I should sleep, but I was lost in the sweet voice. Finally, I did drift away to sleep, floating in his love.

Chapter 12

Pradeep's birthday, 6.07 a.m.

I was filled with enthusiasm. It looked like I was the happiest person on earth. What a wonderful day—the day he was born. It was very special to me. I had told Poo that I would be meeting him alone, and we were going out. She warned me that I was not concentrating on my studies and not attending classes also. I convinced her that I would do well. Now the motto of my life was to keep my Pradeep as happy as possible. I had made all the preparations and plans. Now, it was time to execute them. I called Pradeep over the phone.

'Gooood morning. Happy birthday!'

'How many times will you greet me?'

'Keep counting!' I smiled.

'It's the thirty-seventh time.' He sounded sleepy.

'Want to sleep more?' I didn't want him to!

'Yeah, along with you!' He giggled.

'Idiot! Stop it! You know what? You are the most romantic guy on earth!' I commented, even knowing he was not!

'So true! What time are we meeting? Where are we going?' He was excited.

'Hmm, the weather is also awesome! Everything's turning out to be superb today.' I wished it will.

'May I ask what you are planning?' He really wanted to know the plan.

'Surprise, keep guessing. What are you wearing today?' I wanted to match my dress to what he was going to wear.

'A perfect white on white.' He seems to be up to something.

'All right, see you at nine near the cafe, bye.'

'You know what?'

'What?'

'I lovvvvvve you.'

'You know what I wanted to say?'

'That you love me?'

'Nah, happy birthday.'

'That's the thirty-eighth time!' He smiled, and we both hung up the call. It was going to be the best day of my life. I kept telling myself that I should look my best and went for bath.

I wore a white salwar with lavender border only near the end. The dupatta was also lavender. This dress had a beautiful flare starting from my waist. It had puffs near the shoulders. Pradeep loved this dress. I was looking all fresh with wet hair. I didn't put on any make-up. I just carried all I had planned and left to meet with him.

He sure looked good on white. I saw him walking slowly towards me in his white transparent shirt. He had his arms folded of his shoulders, with some black leather band on his right hand. He was not wearing banyan or T-shirt inside his shirt and had undone his first button. His hair was all curly and wet. I had never seen him dressing so casually—a white shirt, white pants, and some beach-wear sandals. He sure looked like he was attending some beach party! And the funny part was, I guess he had taken his bath today—I meant, at least finally today!

The weather was chilly. It had stopped raining only an hour ago but still cloudy. The cool breeze blew as he was walking towards me. I wanted him with love. As he came near me, he had that million-dollar smile, with a small dimple on his right cheek. He came close.

'Happy birthday, idiot.'

'That's number 39.' He sat behind, without touching me.

'Happy birthday!' I yelled.

'I wish you wish me with a hug and a kiss on my lips.' He smiled.

I gave him a blow on his face and started my vehicle.

'So are we going too far today?' he asked with curiosity.

'Keep guessing!' I drew away.

It was a long ride—an endless ride. I adjusted the mirror so that now and then I could see Pradeep.

He was playing with my back. He kept on writing 'I love you' on my back. He repeatedly asked me to guess what he wrote on my back. I knew it the very first time, but I lied that I didn't know so that he kept on writing on my back.

Buildings began to vanish. We left the city and were moving on the highway. I stopped my vehicle.

'Anything wrong?' he asked, puzzled. I took out my dupatta and turned towards him!

'Not here.' He laughed.

'Stop it, idiot. Close your eyes.' I carefully blindfolded his eyes with my dupatta so that he could not see where I was taking him. This was not pre-planned. I thought I should give him a surprise. I started the vehicle and hit back the road.

'You smell great,' he whispered near my ears, placing his chin on my shoulder. I could not speak a word and kept on riding.

'You know the best part of travelling like this?' he asked me, and I hummed no.

'It's when your hair brushes over my face, and I could smell your sweet aroma.' He sounded too filmy, but I could feel the depth of his voice. I could feel that he actually meant it. I could not react to the beautiful words. I guess I didn't have words for his love. I kept on riding for the next forty-five minutes. I thanked Pleasure for this help to make him get close to me.

My vehicle stopped. He was excited.

'Can I see? Are we in the place you wanted to take me?' He was in a hurry.

'No, you still have a long way to go.' I got down from the vehicle, held his hands, and took him with me. I guided him all the way to the place where I wanted him to come with me. Tiny droplets of water began to pleasure our skin.

'Is it raining?' Pradeep was of no clue as to what he was undergoing.

'Keep walking, only a few minutes more.' I watched out his every step. This moment seemed to be more romantic than what I had actually thought. I was his eyes now. I was leading him to the destination.

'Is that water flowing?' Pradeep was curious every second.

'Don't say anything. Just keep walking.'

'Why is the floor shaking?' He looked scared.

'Relax, my love . . . I'm with you.'

He was holding his hands on each of my shoulders and was walking behind me.

'I guess it's time we both sit,' I told him.

'Can I see now?'

'No, wait. I myself will remove your blindfold.' Both of us sat together. The floor was shaking.

'This is the heaven I wanted to show you.' I told to Pradeep, opening his vision to the beautiful place in front of us.

'Wow, where are we? What is this place?' He sure looked happy, and he loved this place. We were actually sitting on the top of the beautiful river Arkavathi, swinging our legs slightly above the water. It was a wooden hanging bridge, and we were at the centre of the bridge. The trees were covering the entire sides of the river and were a canopy over us, providing us all the privacy on earth. The bridge would shake if we move.

'Liked it?' I expected yes.

'Loved it.' I could see tears in his eyes. He slowly moved over to my shoulders.

'Are you happy?' I knew he was.

'Heaven. I could not ask for a better place to spend time with you. Thank you so much.' He really meant he loved it. We both began to express our love to each other. As our hands held tight together, he slid his palms all the way from my back to the hip and hugged me sideways, pulling me as close as possible. I went resting my head on his chest and began to lose myself for the love.

Chapter 13

Same day, a few hours later

Pradeep broke the silence.

'It's been two hours. We both have been sitting like this. Have you slept?'

'No, I'm enjoying the love.'

'Smritha, can I ask you a few things?' His voice went serious.

'You need my permission? You are my life, Pradeep. Please don't keep these formalities. I have stopped thinking that we both are two separate identities. We are one, dear. Please ask me anything you want.'

'How did it go wrong with your mom?' He wanted to talk about this from a very long time. Every time he spoke about this, I used to change the topic of discussion. Now, I guess I had to tell the truth. The time was here, but his sudden question kept me in a state of shock for the next few seconds. I simply looked at him. For a second, the whole hell came in front of my eyes. The beautiful water flowing under me started to look scary. I started to sweat. I hugged Pradeep out of fear.

I was a baby to him now. I was in his lap. I could see only him and the green trees above him and the little sunshine which broke down the leaf gaps. It was like a light of hope coming to me. I began to tell my mother's life and death to him.

'Pradeep, I have never spoken about this to anyone. But I feel I should share everything with you. My mother was the most beautiful woman on earth. She was tall, fair, and always had dimples on her cheeks. Pradeep, she loved me a lot, and she loved him so much that I can't even tell you how much.' Tears rolled down my eyes right on to his thighs. He wiped them and kissed me on my eyes and expected to know more.

'He was never a good dad to me, Pradeep. He was never a good husband also. Once when I was small of about twelve years, I could see how cruel he really was. He had returned home after a late-night party. I had a high fever, and I was scared to sleep alone in the dark, so mom was with me. He rushed home, and you won't believe how cruelly he reacted.' Another tear rolled off as I remembered the hell from the past.

'Continue, my love.' He was brushing my hair to make me feel better.

'He didn't even bother to see whether I was alive. He rushed in and was trying to touch Mom's lips and squeeze them in front of me. He called her inside his room. Mom never wanted to leave me alone and go. I badly needed her by my side. I was shivering in cold, but he pushed me aside, pulled her by her hand, and dragged her inside the room and locked it. He never loved me or my mother, Pradeep. He only loved having sex with Mom. She was a sex toy to him. My mother came out from the room after a few minutes, full of scratches all over the body. I could see her cry. I could, in fact, see her die every single day. She came and slept with me, trying to make me feel better. Pradeep, you know what? I was just twelve years of age at that time. I couldn't understand many things, but I could understand his greedy intentions and my mother's wetted eyes.'

'Your mother never told this out?' He was touched by her situation.

'No, she loved him, and moreover, everyone knew what my dad was. I'm ashamed to say that he had relationships with many other women. Mom never fought anything against it. She never wanted his reputation to be spoiled. She used to receive only slaps from him whenever she questioned about it. Pradeep, you won't leave me off and go because my dad is not good, right?'

'Don't be idiotic. I love you.'

'I love you too, Pradeep. Please don't leave me for anything. You know what? One unforgettable experience for me was when I was about to experience womanhood for the first time. I was transforming from a girl to a woman. I began to change physically. It was the only day I guess I saw my mom happy. She was so happy. She called all our relatives and shared the happiness. You won't believe me, Pradeep, but I forgot the stomach and back pains, seeing her smile. She had those beautiful dimples. Those were very rare, and I would have endured any amount of pain just to see those beautiful dimples on her face.' My face began to smile, remembering that moment.

'How did she die?' He was at the lowest voice tone.

'It was the worst day of my life, Pradeep. In fact, I was hoping and wishing that that day would bring back happiness in my mother's life, but it turned out to be her last day. I could only see fights between them. Every day and every night were just fights. Only fights remained between them, and every time, Dad won. The only thing remained for Mom was tears. That day, surprisingly, he came to me and started speaking nicely. He showed Mom love without lust for the first time. He apologized to me and her as well. He told her that he would keep her happy. He told her that he would leave all his other illegal relationships and be loyal to her. He told her that he wanted her love. It was an emotional day for us. The three of us ate together. He opened his bag and showed a tour package to us. He told us that he wanted to start a new life, and the best way to begin was with a holiday. He left Mom and me to choose the place for the holiday. Trust me, Pradeep, that was the first time all three of us went out together. In fact, it turned out to be the last. I chose Kerala. Mom was also happy and excited. She was hoping for a new beginning.' My hands slightly went sliding on Pradeep's chest and all the way to his cheeks. I brushed his hair, and my forefinger delicately ran over his lips. He kissed my finger, and I began to speak again.

'We had a neighbour who runs tourism business. In fact, he himself was a cab driver. He is a weird guy, Pradeep. He always used to talk to me with care. He used to bring chocolates when I was young. We decided to go in his car as he was also a good friend of our family. I was seated at the back with Mom, and Uncle Sam was accompanied by dad in the front seat. Oh! I forgot . . . his name was Samuel, and I used to call him Uncle Sam. We left our home at night nine o'clock, hoping to see the sunrise tomorrow in Kerala. Uncle Sam was a superb driver. Every now and then, he used to halt for a coffee nearby small dabas, coffee shops, and all. He brought me so much to eat at that unusual time. I used to taste hot omelettes at roadside cafes late at night. It was awesome. And soon my position changed from the back seat to the front seat. Both Mom and Dad were sleeping at back, and Uncle Sam was giving me all the entertainment I wanted. Soon I slept. I was woken up by the thin sunlight of Kerala, and a warm smile of Uncle Sam followed it, Pradeep . . . It sure was the place of God. Thick green, no matter where you look. Long empty roads, tall coconut trees, and every now and then, I saw people, and they all were wearing white. That sure was heaven. In fact, that was the first time I had ever gone out with my family.'

Pradeep was watching me with love. I remembered the love showed by Mom. His love was as expressive as Mom's. I closed my eyes, taking a deep breath and started to speak again.

'Uncle Sam had arranged for everything. Everything went on so nicely. Our Kerala stay, food, and nature . . . I loved them all, and surprisingly, Dad told me that he would take me to the beach. I was on cloud nine, Pradeep. I have seen beaches only on television. I was dying to reach there. Uncle Sam took us to the private beach of his friend's place. I would spend my entire life there! It was sooo beautiful . . . I could see so much water, and I could see is a huge ship somewhere at the horizon. I checked my Pinku. It was around five in the evening. Sky was turning red. I could see glimpses of blue and golden brown. I could see the colours coming back into my life as the sun started to shrink into the deep blue sea. I noticed the huge ship fluctuating. It was a beautiful scene. That's the last time I admired the beauty of the ocean. I remembered Poo's words: "Beauty is the outer face of cruelty."

'The waves were becoming huge. I never realized it was a sign of danger—not any one of us did. I could no longer see the ship. I guess it crossed the horizon. I was thinking about my physics classes. Now I understand what LOS is. It means "line of sight". I think nature has so much which we should learn. Suddenly the waves began to become huge. Uncle Sam asked me to step back from the water. I noticed the water level rising. The waves which kissed me a few minutes back were now wetting my knees. Uncle Sam told the three of us that he had never seen the ocean being so rude. I corrected him immediately that it was a sea, not an ocean. He patted me on my shoulders and appreciated my geographical skills, and we all smiled at one other. Then we went to the nearest resort and were watching the sunset from a sufficient height. Uncle Sam was telling his experience in Kumbla and Mahe beaches. Mom and Dad were lost in their own romantic world. I was so happy to see them like this, and I turned to the other side, to the sea, and was chatting with Uncle Sam.

'I wanted to tell all these to Poo. I had taken so many pictures, and I have to show her so much. I wish she were here.'

Pradeep woke me up. 'Here? What are you saying?'

'I don't know, Pradeep . . . I was literally there now. I guess as I closed my eyes, my entire soul went back there!'

'Close your eyes and imagine you are there and tell me everything.' My actions followed his voice . . .

'I called Poo from Uncle Sam's phone, facing away from the sea, and was telling her the beauty of the water. The beauty of its colours. The ultimate beauty of nature. Suddenly I was pushed by someone, and I fell down. The phone slipped from my hand. Water seemed to be everywhere. I realized that someone who pushed me was a huge wave. My eyes were blinded by water. I could hear only water. I couldn't breathe. I tried to breathe through my mouth, but I tasted an extremely high amount of salt. I began to choke. Water was everywhere, Pradeep. It was hell.' I started choking and woke up. My eyes were red and filled with tears. I sat down, wiping my tears, and took a deep breath and looked at Pradeep.

'Relax, Smritha, you are safe in my arms. Come here.' His arms spread wide open and wrapped around me.

'Pradeep, I don't remember what happened next. The last thing I remember was Uncle Sam handing me over to Dad, and he ran to the sea again. I soon became unconscious. Later in the hospital, I noticed Dad. He didn't have a tear in his eyes. I asked him about Mom and Uncle Sam. He spontaneously told me that they both are dead and their bodies are already buried. I looked around me. There were a huge number of injured people. Dad told me that it was a tsunami. I couldn't pronounce it properly at the first time. I burst into tears. I screamed, cried hard, but I couldn't see my mom. I yelled and cursed God. I thought everything was getting better, but it was the end of Mom's life, not the beginning of her new life. He told me that I was unconscious for the past four days and he had arranged for our return back home and we would leave once my health became still better. I could not believe how I survived. Doctors rushed when they heard me yelling. They spoke the language which I could never understand. All I could hear was the word *relax.*' Then I was silent, waiting for Pradeep's reaction.

'Then you came back and joined this college?' He was still embracing me tightly.

'Yeah, Pradeep. Do you know why I still hate my father?'

'Because he didn't cry when your mom died?'

'No . . . He was unpredictable. We had returned home after experiencing the hell on earth. All my relatives were consoling me. Everyone started to praise Mom in their own words. I heard from them all the possible good words. Few cried along with me, but soon, everyone was gone and I was all alone with Dad. I was not comfortable with him. I wanted a shoulder to cry on. I wanted someone to console me. Obviously, dad was not an option. In the afternoon that day, I went to Poo's house, telling Dad that I would sleep over Poo's place. I was narrating to her the entire story. She made me feel better. She started telling that my dad has changed and I should love him. After seeing the love he showed to

Mom, I had developed a soft corner for him. My Pinku was showing nine thirty in the evening. I told her I will sleep with Dad as he might be feeling alone. I guess that was the first time I thought about his happiness, and I rushed home. The door was locked. I thought he might have slept. I didn't want to disturb him. I used my key and entered home. I thought I should check him once before going to sleep. I knew Dad was a strong man, but he might be crying alone. So I decided to go and console him and then go to sleep. I went to his room. I was stunned, Pradeep. I saw him in a compromising position with some lady. I felt disgusted. I felt ashamed. I wished I should not have born to this man. I just ran back to Poo's house and slept there that night.'

Pradeep sure looked shocked by what I had told him today. My story was sure an adventurous mystery, but there lies a deep pain within—the pain of losing a loving mom, the pain of having a shameful dad. I spoke again.

'Pradeep, I'm not like my dad. Do you trust me? You love me, right?' I looked deep into his eyes.

'I know what you are, my love. I love you more than anything in this world. Hmmm, now tell me, how much do you love yourself?'

'Myself? Hmmm . . . I don't know.'

'I love you more than you love yourself, understood?' Silence reigned for the next few minutes. It was already two. My Pinku sure ran fast in situations like this. We both walked to where we parked our vehicle. I began to speak.

'I have a surprise for you.'

'What? Another one? What's that?'

'Open my Pleasure's seat. You have the surprise there.' His eyes were happy. He was excited. He was pleading for the key. I placed the key end in between my lips and asked him to take the key himself. I wished he would brush my lips while taking the key. I wanted the delicate skin of my lips be pleasured by his fingers. Pradeep looked around. The place was reserved. He locked my hands with his hands and came close to me. His lips grabbed the other end of the key and pulled the key out of my control. Our lips didn't even touch each others, but I got goosebumps as his lips were so near to mine. I stepped back and shook my head and pinched Pradeep near his arm and said, 'You have become naughty nowadays!'

A smile followed, and he ran to the vehicle to see what was in it. I had arranged for this for hours. Every girl on earth gets happiness if she receives gifts from her man. She feels happy if she is treated special, but I love to make him special. Pradeep opened it up. Two small red heart-shaped hydrogen-filled balloons flew away as he opened it. He tried to catch them.

'Let them go . . . That's the announcement to the world that our hearts are united.' He smiled and saw a lot of roses—blood-red roses.

'Count them, Pradeep,' I whispered.

He began to slowly count every rose. He noticed a glass lid covering something. He kept on counting flowers, and he picked up the last flower.

'That's number 143, right?' I looked deep into those happy eyes.

'And that says "I love you", right?'

'You are never wrong, Pradeep. Open the lid. That's for you.' Pradeep held all 143 flowers in his left hand and opened the glass lid which covered his surprise.

'This is beautiful.' He kept looking at the very tiny small piece of cake which is in the shape of a heart. It was completely covered with strawberry sauce. He took out the cake and looked at me.

'This sure is beautiful, but I can't cut it. Can we share it the way we played with the key?' There was a naughty smile over his face.

'Idiot, stop it. I can't do that. I held the piece and let him have the first bite, wishing him a happy birthday, and later we both fed each other until it was no more.

'That's number 41. How many times do you want to greet me?'

'The magic number 143.' We soon left for home, and I kept my word that day.

Chapter 14

One month later

Everything was not the same as it was a month ago. Study holidays were declared as it was one month to go before the exams. Every now and then, we would go to the college to write preparatory exams. Pradeep started avoiding me with an excuse of studying for the exams. It was days since we saw each other. Casual phone calls and messages were the only means of contact. In fact, I knew somewhere within me that he was truly studying hard and all his hard work was only for our bright future, but I really missed him. I started feeling lonely. Even Poo got busy with her studies, but I seriously couldn't understand why I was not able to study. Every time I sat to study, I would always get lost in thoughts. I would be daydreaming. My thoughts would be baseless. I would assume myself to have studied everything and would spend loads of time dreaming about Pradeep and me. The number of sheets of paper which I used to plan my timetable to study was more than the number of sheets which I used for studying!

Every day new timetable was formed and new hopes of studying arrived. Dad bought me a new laptop. I guess he was trying to please me. He told me that it would help out in my studies. I slowly began being active on social sites. My laptop was connected to the Internet using my phone. Making new friends and chatting continued endlessly. I kept myself busy in order to overcome my loneliness. Once or twice I even had a friendly chat with Amar but didn't go too personal. Neither did he stay online for long.

It was a boring evening. I was lying down on my bed. Finally, Pradeep called up.

'Hello, dear, studying hard?'

'Can we please talk about something other than studies?'

'Really? I heard your neighbours were complaining that you were singing about product rule and different laws of physics even when you bathe.' He was laughing.

'Very funny, but I'm not laughing.' I seriously didn't like the joke.

'Hmm . . . won't you ask why on earth did I call so suddenly?'

'You need reasons to call me?'

'Not like that, my sweet Smritha . . . Why are you so angry?'

'Then what do you expect me to be? You can't even spend time with me.'

'Look, Smritha. I may not be chatting with you all the time or meeting you daily, but the magnitudes of our love will never disintegrate.'

'Will you stop using scientific words, at least when we talk about love?'

'All right, forget it. I was thinking about you for a few minutes, so I called you to say something.'

'Finally! All right go on.'

'You remember the day of my birthday? The most beautiful day of my life?' My anger reduced slowly, hearing his sweet voice.

'I can never ever forget that day.'

'Neither can I. Actually, do you remember when those tears rolled down from those beautiful eyes, I wiped them and kissed those eyes?' His voice grew romantic, which started to melt me up.

'Yeah, how can I forget such a golden moment of my life?' My voice was softened.

'I was wondering how come your tears were so sweet, and finally, when I was thinking about it, I found the answer.'

'Why, dear?' I knew he would say something romantic.

'Every time I wiped your tear, I guess it was not the only thing I wiped. I was also wiping your nose.' And then he blasted immediately and started to laugh aloud.

'I will kill you. You are disgusting.' I was now laughing with him.

'Finally, the mystery of sweet tear came to an end.' He was still laughing.

'Nothing like that. It was my tear only.'

'Smritha, I love you.' Thank God, I finally heard those three words which I was waiting from days.

'Love you, Pradeep. Love you sooooooo much that you can't even imagine how much. Please don't avoid me.' My voice turned out to be serious.

'I was not avoiding you, my love. I'm doing all these for our future. You can understand it, right?'

'My brain can! But not my heart.'

'Use only your brain, study well. After one and a half month, let's party hard. Now study well, all right?' I smiled.

'Yeah, study well. I have to study the topic on crystal lattice. I will call you later. Love you, bye.' He hung up.

I was very happy after that chat. I took up the textbook, and after a long gap, I finally read something helpful.

Chapter 15

The next day, around nine thirty

I woke up with the great feeling of having studied well last night. After all, it was a sign of satisfaction. I checked my mobile. I could not find any message from Pradeep. I told to myself, 'As expected,' and saw Poo's message. I didn't open it, thinking that it would be just a forwarded message. I threw the mobile on the bed and went to check the so-called other human at home. No sign of him at home. I went to the kitchen to have some coffee, but something pulled me to check out what Poo had sent. I went back to my room and checked Poo's message.

'I wish I were you, Smritha. I'm fed up of this life.'

I could not believe the words. I had never seen Poo becoming so emotional. I always used to share all my pain with her since childhood, but I never heard about her pains. She had good, decent parents, and she did not love anyone. When there was no love, there might be no pain, I guess. I checked the time of delivery. It was at 2 a.m. I wondered what she was doing late at night.

I called her. 'Hello, are you home?' I spoke as soon as she received the call.

'Yeah. Why?' She sounded sleepy.

'What happened, Poo?' I tried to be polite.

'Nothing, I will call you later. I'm sleepy, bye.' She hung up without waiting for me to say bye.

I guess she might have stressed out because of all these studies, but still I wanted to talk to her. I went online to check out my Facebook profile. There was nothing special. I left for Poo's place.

Everything seemed to be normal—from her mother to Uncle Murthy. All seemed to be smiling and welcomed me home. I went to her room; it was not locked. I went in. She was sleeping like a baby. Her cheeks were baby pink. Her lips were so tender. She locked so fresh and delicate. I could not go further. I wanted her to sleep. I turned back and started to go out.

'Why are you going back?' she whispered.

'Are you awake?' I was shocked.

'Yeah. I am lying on my bed, but I can't fall asleep.'

'What happened, Poo? Scared of the exams?' I provoked her to speak.

'Nah . . . Nothing wrong, I'm all right.'

'What's that message all about?'

'What message?'

I showed her my inbox. She was shocked to see it.

'Oh, I sent you that? I don't remember properly, Smritha. I was very sleepy, and yeah, I'm scared of the exams, so I sent you a message like that.' I knew she was lying to me. I could easily tell that she was lying, but I didn't want to put up an argument and just smiled at her.

'I will study with you today.' I smiled.

'Really? Where are the books?'

'I will share yours. Let's study together.' I wanted to spend time with her. At least then she could say something which was in her.

'Did you brush your teeth?' She smiled.

'Yeah. Why?'

'Then what's stopping you to smile. Say cheese.' She was so sweet.

In no time there was a smile in my face.

'Smritha, we can't share the same book. Do one thing. Get the biology and mathematics books. Do you have class notes?'

'Yeah, but it's incomplete.'

'How can anyone expect it to be complete when you didn't even attend classes? Go home and get a few rough sheets, your incomplete notes, and also the Bosco publications textbook. Let's start working out today. I have also run out of working sheets, so get me some too . . . I mean, while I take a bath, do pooja, and will be ready to start, all right?' She walked away.

I left for my house. I was riding slowly as the road was slippery due to rain last night. My Pinku was ticking eleven. I was wearing a sleeveless T-shirt and a three-quarter length pants which were contrasting in colour. Suddenly I felt strange. Someone just kissed on my shoulder. I felt chilly on that spot, and another kiss was soon followed on my other shoulder. Now it was thousands of kisses coming on all over my body. I loved the love behind these kisses. It was the love of nature. Yes, the things which kissed me were raindrops. Tiny droplets of Mother Nature made me feel so good. Soon I was drenched. I couldn't see the road. It was raining heavily. I pulled over and stood under a shade on the side of the road. The road sure looked empty, but I guess I was wrong. I saw him. A tight-fit T-shirt which was wet hugged his body, and he was showcasing his manly muscles. Yes, it was Amar. He stood up from his bike and walked towards me. I was thrilled and waited for him to start the conversation.

'How come you are here? Had been to Poo's house?' He had a naughty smile.

'How come you know her house is nearby?' I was winking with a smile.

'I have seen her nearby this place many times. I live at the place very near from here.'

'It's so funny, right? We never spoke directly when we were together in the college, and now we are speaking as if we have been friends for ages.' I expected a smile.

'Yeah. Then how are you studying? Started reviewing the topics?'

'I didn't even complete reading a single subject,' I posted the truth.

'How is Pooja? You spoke to her?'

'Yeah, I did. She was sleeping. Now, I will go back to her house after taking some books. We will read together today.'

'That's sounds better. Then I guess I have to go home. Hmmm, I will catch you later. He started his bike and moved away. I was so thrilled. Our first meeting couldn't have been better, but as it was our first talk, we could not be free with each other. I felt so free when I chatted with him, but now when we spoke directly, I could not develop chemistry well. The word *chemistry* reminded me about something. I shouldn't be standing alone like this. I needed to move towards home. I guess I cannot return back to Poo as the rain seemed not to stop. I decided to study by myself today and left for home.

Pinku was telling me that it was lunchtime. I changed my dress and had my lunch alone. I called up Poo and told her that I would read today on my own and sat in front of the TV. I switched on to a music video channel. A hot Bollywood number was showing a romantic scene. I switched on to a bolder channel and searched the channel list to find anything romantic. I could not find any. It had been long since I grew romantic. Pradeep didn't have time to romance with me. I was haunted with loneliness. Amar's body made me go mad now. I told to myself to study. I called up Pradeep. He never picked up. I called him almost five times, but he never responded. I guess he was studying with his cell phone in silent mode. I was feeling very lonely. I went online and logged on to the networking site where Amar and I had spoken up once privately. I wish he would come online. I was waiting for him. Finally, the wait ended when I got a reply from Amar.

'It's been so long since the last time we spoke.'

'Few hours is long?'

'Even a minute is long!'

'Amar, you looked stunning when your body hugged your wet shirt. Superb.'

I was shocked by how easily I started talking freely with him. Probably as I was in a romantic mood, I started off quickly I guess.

'You liked the shirt?'

'Yeah, I loved it. Then how are you studying? How much did you finish studying in biology?'

'I'm through with the last unit.'

'You mean human reproduction?'

'Yeah.'

'Looks like your personal experience might have helped you out to study it well.' I could not believe that I had become so close to him all of a sudden. I could speak anything with him.

'No, I still don't have any such experience. Do you have?'

'I don't even speak much with boys. Then how can I have such experience?'

'Hmmm . . . Then you mean to say that there is nothing between you and Pradeep?'

This was a bit serious question. I never wanted to remember Pradeep when I was like this.

'No, we are just friends. Who told you that we are going around?' I was tense.

'It's an open secret you know? Everyone says so.'

'No, Amar, I don't love him. He proposed to me many times, but I always rejected him.' I never wanted to speak like this, but at this moment, I wanted to be close with Amar. Pradeep had left me alone for days. I needed someone to share my thoughts with, and it could be Amar. I didn't want Pradeep to come between our romantic chat. At least for now.

'Really? Then I'm sorry. I spoke without knowing the truth. Then what are you doing?'

'Just lying down all alone and feeling soooo much alone.' I expected him to go romantic and speak like he wanted me.

'Then do you like me joining you there?' He was brave enough to start up. I knew it was wrong, but I was all alone all these days. I needed some love. This was just a secret fantasy. I could chat with him like this online. It would not be like I was cheating on Pradeep. I loved him, but for now, this lust was beautiful.

'Hmm . . .' I nodded.

'All right, imagine you and me all alone in a beautiful beach. The tide is low, and it's very calm. It is blue all around us. I am wearing white shorts and a white transparent shirt, while you are wearing a white shirt which is so large that it extends till your knees.'

He made me sweat—not romantically, but out of fear. I never felt the place romantic as I don't like the beach.

'Amar, I love the dress we both are wearing, but please change the location. I can't imagine romance near the water. Can it be somewhere else?' I said softly.

'Of course. Anywhere you want to. We can romance anywhere on earth, and even beyond earth.' He tried to be sexy.

'Can it be in some room?' I wanted it to be more private.

'Yeah, it can be in my room. My room's theme is white—the walls, the floor, the bed. In fact, everything in it is white. You are in an extra-large red synthetic satin shirt.' He made me imagine myself at that place.

'And . . .' I pleaded.

'And you are sleeping on my bed, like a baby. I will come walking towards you and will sit next to you.' He sent it with a blushing emoticon followed by a kissing emoticon.

'And? Please continue,' I pleaded for more.

'You pretend to be asleep. My fingertip slowly brushes the outline of your lips, and I will move the hair covering your ears.'

'Ears? Why?' I was breathing harder with my eyes closed, assuming that the things were actually happening.

'I will tell you why. Hmmm . . . I guess I shouldn't just tell you. You will realize it yourself. Now, I move close to your ears and whisper "Smritha" and try to wake you up.'

'And . . .' It was getting romantic.

'And I kiss you on your ear, but you still pretend to be asleep. Now my lips move away from your ear, brushing your cheek, and then near to your lips.' His imagination was beyond my expectation.

'Am I still sleeping?' I tried to behave innocent.

'No! You are not! You pretend to be asleep. You want me to love you more,' he replied with a kissing emoticon.

'Then love me more. What are you waiting for?' I demanded.

'I will use my mouth to remove the first button of your shirt, and . . .' He paused.

'Oh my god! Please continue. You are too romantic!' I exclaimed.

The romantic chat continued for the next one hour. He excited me to an extent that I have never experienced before, and we both reached orgasm.

Chapter 16

Next day, 3 a.m.

I was alone in the dark. I had a knife in my hand. Everything seemed to be dark. I was locked up. There were no doors to exit, not even windows which would make me breathe. I was scared, scared of my own footsteps. I was all alone, not even my shadow was with me. I decided to end it all. Mom was calling me. The only way to go now was to her. My nerves were cut. I was killing myself. I was wobbling on the floor. I sat up, holding my wrist. I looked around. The room was not dark indeed, and I was not on the floor. I had just woken up from one of the worst nightmares I ever dreamt.

'What have I done?' I told to myself. I was proving to be his daughter. I was cheating over my love. I hated this lust. It was that feeling. I want it to get away from me. I was ashamed. I walked out of the bedroom and into the washroom. Pinku was ticking three in the morning. I switched on the light and stood in front of the mirror. My Pinku's tick-tock sound was scaring me. I threw her on the bed from the restroom. I saw my own face in the mirror. It had never looked so ugly. I was ugly—not from the outside, but deep inside me, I was ugly. I splashed water on to my face and looked up again. The water did not make me look better. I could see a girl who landed up cheating on her love just for pleasure, and sex seemed to be the most disgusting thing on earth to me. I wanted to wash off my sins. I went under the shower. Water flowed all over my body, but it was not taking away my guilt. It was not taking away the ugly part of me as it used to do before.

I started to find answers to my questions under the shower. Wasn't this cheating? Wasn't this the worst thing that a girl can do to her trusting love? I guess I didn't do something which was not forgivable. I didn't go physical with Amar. I just found the romantic part of Pradeep in Amar. It was just a chat, a romantic chat, and it was over. I didn't lose anything. I still remained pure. No one other than my love had touched me. It was just a matter of lust. I tried to get over my loneliness with a sex chat. I was still pure. Yes, I was pure.

Was I pure? No, I was not. It was not just the physical which was of importance. I was impure from the heart. I loved Pradeep, but when he was not around me, I went for other options. After all, Pradeep was struggling hard to make our future secure, but instead of supporting him in his efforts, I was finding my fantasies and enjoying myself. What if Pradeep came to know about this? What if Amar leaked it out to the world? I kept on asking myself questions—questions which I had no answers, questions for which I had no explanation to prove my innocence. I was down.

It was no use of me sitting under the water shower. Water seemed of no help to wash my guilt this time. I decided to call Pradeep and confess the truth. I came out of the washroom, water dripping off my body. I changed to dry clothes. I took up the phone. I didn't know whether what I was doing was right or not, but I sure wanted to kill this guilt, and finally I called him.

'Hello. Woke up so early?' His voice had freshness. I couldn't speak. I went down on my knees. I burst into tears.

'What happened? Why are you crying?' He had so much concern in his voice.

'I . . . I . . . I don't know.' I couldn't speak. I was scared to confess the truth. It was the ugly truth. He might hate me. He might leave me. He might never come back to me.

'You need not tell anything. I can understand. Don't worry. Things will be fine. You will do well in the exams. Did you sleep last night? Hmm . . . I guess you didn't . . . You are so scared of the exams. Now relax.' I was feeling so guilty. Pradeep was so innocent. He thought I was worried about the exams, but I never bothered about it. I was selfish.

'I . . .' I tried to start.

'Don't say anything, my love. My shoulder is waiting for you to rest on it. Come on now. You need some rest.' His voice was so soft and was full of love. I hugged my pillow, imagining it was him. I could feel his love—pure love without lust.

'Now, close your eyes like a good girl, leaving behind all the pains and problems. You are safe in these arms now. Just relax, my love. Take a deep breath and roll to the sweet sleep which gives those tiny little eyes some rest.' My actions followed his words. I found myself in his arms in my imagination. I was lost in love. I never realized when he made me drift away into the most peaceful sleep on earth.

Chapter 17

Two months later, eleven o'clock in the morning

Finally, the hell was over. I finished off my exams. Nothing seemed to have happened in the last two months. I became quite serious about studies. The guilt inside me made me study well. I wanted to prove to Pradeep that I could score well and would be a huge support to him. I never went online since that day. Life would be normal from now on. Pradeep would spend more time with me. I didn't do the exams that well, and the entrance exam was not a piece of cake. But still I was sure I would land up in some college to complete my engineering course. Hopes were now high. I had prayed to every god I knew (including Mom) for my results to be fine, hoping for things to turn on my way.

Pradeep was planning to leave for his home town to meet up with his mother. He promised me that he would come back soon, and we both could have a blast. He was going tomorrow, so I should have a long conversation with him before he left for his place. We had planned to meet up in a coffee shop at this time. I had been waiting for him for the past half an hour. Cute idiot, he would never be on time. Someone patted me on the back.

'Searching for someone?' He was smiling.

'When will you learn to be on time? You made me wait for so long . . . Hate you.' I pretended to be angry.

'I know . . .' His reactions were only smiles.

We both walked into the cafe. I was seeing some changes in Pradeep. His care had reduced. He only cared about me only when I was down. I guess it was just sympathy. I felt the love was falling down, or he might have become more practical. I made myself comfortable on the chair. Pradeep sat in front of me.

'You don't love me any more,' I murmured.

'What made you say that?' He raised her eyebrows.

'You don't care for me as you used to do before.'

'Is love all about caring? Remember once I had told you about love graph? The magnitude of love is on y-axis and time is on x-axis. So the magnitude of love should increase linearly with respect to time. If the slope becomes infinity, then a sudden drop occurs.' He smiled.

'But yours is decreasing linearly,' I fired back.

'It's not decreasing, sweetheart. Look, soon after the exams, I can't raise the slope from horizontal halt state to vertical raise. Give me some time.' He seemed to be in the exam mood still.

'Will you please stop speaking technically? I'm fed up of those words.' I was irritated.

'Look, Smritha. We need to sit and plan our future, and we will do that when I come back from my place, all right?' I wondered why on earth had he become so serious, but I respected his maturity.

'I love you, Pradeep. I will be missing you. Come back soon. I had enough of these exams. I seriously want to spend some quality time with you. Hope you can understand my concern and love,' I pleaded to my sweetheart.

'Yes, my princess. I also want to come back soon. When I come back, make sure you have found places like the one you found for my birthday.' He winked at me. I began to blush at his wink.

Pradeep and I spoke for a few moments more before he left for his home town. I came back home, and all of a sudden, life seemed so boring. We had no work on holidays, and I couldn't do any better work other than sleep. But at this age, you couldn't expect more sleep also. Poo had invited me for lunch.

I checked out my Pinku. She reminded me to leave for her place. I wanted to be with her and decided to go for dinner and sleep with her. It had been long since we both slept together.

Chapter 18

Same day, 11 p.m.

I rolled to my right, and Poo was thinking something deeply. I wondered about studies.

'What's wrong with you? Feeling bad because the exams got over?' I giggled. She didn't laugh, not even a smile.

'You know what? Every morning in the jungle, a gazelle wakes up, and it knows it must run faster than the fastest lion in the forest, or it will get killed. Every morning a lion wakes up, and it knows it must outrun the slowest gazelle, or it will starve to death. It does not matter whether you are a lion or a gazelle. When the sun comes up, you better start running.' She said it, looking at the ceiling fan seriously.

'Are you mad? What's this lion–gazelle story?' I was confused.

'You can analyze this in two ways. Can you guess?' She was still staring up.

'You all right?' I didn't find her so serious very often, so I was wondering what was bothering her.

'You can never think so deeply . . . Let me tell you. The first way is to look at it as a short explanation of a student's life. The society is the lion. This society includes parents, friends, teachers, relatives, and all. And the gazelle is the student. Every morning we have to wake up, and we should run. Here, *run* means *studies*. If we run slowly, the society will kill us with its cruel words, so we need to keep running.' She had a sarcastic smile on her face.

'And the second analysis is?' I asked.

'I can't tell you, forget it.' She closed her delicate eyes slowly.

'Please don't sleep. Wake up.' I started tapping her on her abdomen region.

'All right. Look, in the second view, the gazelle is a girl, and the lion is a boy. The word *running* has two different meanings—one for the gazelle and the other for the lion. For the gazelle, *run* means the action of not falling in love, and for the lion it's action of dragging the gazelle into its love. It does not matter if the gazelle runs slow or the lion runs fast. Finally, the gazelle will be killed.' She paused.

'So you mean to say, if a girl can't resist or the boy loves her too much, then they both will fall in love, and the girl will be killed?' I was trying to put the whole jungle story in a straightforward way.

'Exactly . . .' She was still closing her eyes.

'So how can you say that the girl will be killed? She can live happily with him, right?' I went close to her.

'Shall we sleep now?' she murmured.

'Poo, I'm your friend. You can share things with me.' I smiled.

'Just shut up. You remembered it now? Your life is full of that Pradeep. Every day, every second, you think about him. Whenever you come to me, you always speak about him. Till now you couldn't find out my problems. You are just using me as a personal diary. You dump all your emotions. At least once, have you come to me and asked me what I underwent? That day when I texted you that I wanted to share something with you, you just came in and went back. You never care about me. Now why the hell are you asking? Just because you don't have anything to do and he is not around? I hate you, Smritha.' She woke up, turned to the other side, and started to cry. I couldn't believe my own eyes. Was what I was seeing actually what I was seeing? Was this Poo who was sparking? She never had spoken to me like this.

'But you never told me anything. What happened, Poo? I thought you are all right as you never told me anything.' I rested my hand on her right shoulder.

'That's what you think, Smritha. If I don't speak or share anything, it does not mean that I don't have any problem. It means that I'm crying inside. You know what? Every smile is a lie. Every laugh is fake. It's all because I'm crying inside and don't want my tears to show. Sorry, Smritha. Please sleep now. We will speak tomorrow.' She stood up and walked away. I stopped her by holding her left hand. She turned back. Her eyes were red. Her cheeks were wet. She looked at me for love.

'I made her sleep on my lap and started to brush her hair. Her tears seemed not to stop. She was not crying, but tears were flowing silently from her eyes. This continued for the next few minutes.

'What happened, Poo? Did Uncle tell you anything?' I kept my voice as soft as possible.

'They didn't, Smritha. That's the problem. They both are so sweet. In my childhood, Dad got me everything before I could ask for them on my birthday. He would come with a beautiful gift. Even now he treats me like a baby, and Mom has been so nice . . . You know her. Till now she has not scolded me hard. Not even once she has slapped me. Such great parents, Smritha . . . I'm lucky to have them.'

I wiped the tears off her cheeks.

'Trust me, Poo. You sure are lucky. Then what is killing you?' I was still brushing her hair.

'Love, Smritha, love. I'm going mad . . .' She started to cry harder. I was stunned. I could not believe my ears.

'Love? Poo, I do not understand anything. Make it clear. Look, it's not just your problem. I will do anything for my Poo to smile. Let's find solution for it together. Now, tell me clearly what happened.' I looked straight into her eyes.

'Who else can I share my problems with, Smritha? I will, but not now. Please don't force me.' She turned to the other side on my lap.

'It's now or never. I want to know what is hurting my best friend.' I was not going to leave her until I knew the truth.

'All right then. Smritha, actually he loves me so much. The more I know about his love, the more I want to have him in my life. I'm trying to find the depth of his love, but it's so deep. The more I discover, the more is left undiscovered. He cares about me so much. One small hurt, one little scratch in my body will bring tears in his eyes. He loves me more than any guy could love his girl on this planet.' She smiled.

'Who is he?' I was quick with the question.

'Don't ask his name, Smritha . . . Every day he calls me up to check out whether I'm okay. Every morning he starts up his day seeing my face first.'

'Face?' I interrupted.

'I mean photo. He has my photo in his cell. He keeps looking at it, it seems. At two or three in the morning, he texts me about how beautiful I am . . . It means he must be looking at my photo late at night, right?' She looked at my eyes.

'This might be a few days' attraction, Poo.' I moved my palm on her cheeks.

'Such attraction does not remain for years. For almost one and half years, he has loved me in a huge scale. I found it to be increasing and never did it decrease.'

'What? One and half years? I didn't even have a clue about it, Poo.

'Even now you shouldn't have . . . but I'm telling you this only because I believe you can understand me.'

'Yeah, I will. How did it happen?' I was the most curious girl on earth.

'You know me, right, Smritha? I don't even have contact with boys. I speak to Pradeep for your sake, but other than him, I don't speak with any one of the guys in the college. But one day something unusual happened. He came into my life. Let me make it clear to you that I have not accepted him even now—not even once have I said that I love him. But he never forgets to tell me how much he loves me every single day. First, I decided that I should be his friend and change his love into friendship, but now I fear of changing my friendship into love.' She looked tense.

Why didn't you avoid him just the way you normally do to people who come to you for love?' I looked puzzled.

'He is different. I could not hurt him. I just wanted him to forget about love and start a new life. So I'm trying to change him.'

'That's stupidity . . . If you do so, then it will increase, Poo. Do you like him?'

'Yeah, I like him, but can't tell you that I love him. Smritha, will you listen to what I say? I feel like sharing it with you now.' She looked so innocent.

'Sure, dear. Speak out,' I begged.

'He is so thoughtful, Smritha. He comes in front of my house just to see me for a few seconds. He loves me so much. He encourages me with my hidden talents. Remember I had stopped painting long back? He recently presented me an entire painting set, from colours to brushes of all sizes. He tries to bring back my happiness in my life. He doesn't want me to sacrifice my happiness for anything. A year back, he made me join a painting workshop. Believe it or not, he used to come and watch how I do, leaving all his work. You know my parents always wanted marks. They wanted me to study. They never bothered about my likes and dislikes. They are concerned about their reputation. But this guy used to come there, encourage me and make me feel better. He also asked me not to tell Mom or Dad about these classes and workshop. He took care of me like a dad.' She finally paused and looked at my shocked face.

'Are you so much attached to him?' I kept my voice low so her parents don't hear me.

'Yeah, beyond your imagination. I love his voice on the phone. I lose myself for him. His voice will resonate inside me even when he keeps his cell phone down. You know what? I'm addicted to him. Every night he makes me sleep, leaving all my stress. Whenever we can't talk, like at times when you sleep with me or when Mom sleeps with me, we both spend sleepless nights thinking about each other,' she whispered.

'It looks like you love him.'

'No, I don't. Look, Smritha, life is not as simple as you think. *Love* is an impossible word to me.'

'Are you mad? You seriously love him. Accept it. If he truly loves you so much, then you are lucky. You will have such a beautiful life.' I begin to smile.

'When I'm with him, I forget everything. I feel that I don't want anything other than him, but when I come back home and see my dad's face, the guilt kills me. I realize that I don't love him. Dad trusts me so much. He has been hurt so much in his part by his family. Now I can't even try to make a small pain in his life. I want the rest of his life to be heaven.' Her tears began to roll off again.

'So you are struck between him and your dad? Maybe we can convince Uncle, right?' I sounded convincing to myself.

'It's not as easy as you think, Smritha. Every time they speak about my arranged marriage, I feel the fear of losing him, but still I have decided that I will hurt myself and sacrifice him. Let me tell you something, Smritha. A person loving someone even though he knows he won't be loved back is whom I call a pure lover. And that's him. Till now, I never felt anything other than love in his touch. His love is so pure. I'm not lucky to take it, Smritha.' She cried harder.

'Stop it. You might wake up Uncle or Auntie. Now tell me who he is. Let's try to solve it.' I was badly curious to know such a good, loving boy.

'No, nothing is going to be solved. My first love will end before it could start. I will be married to some rich guy in the future. I should see hell with him, and the parents will be happy.' She slept on the bed.

'Please.' I shook her, holding her arms.

'Look, Smritha, that's the end. Your nightmare is over, and tomorrow you are not going to ask anything about this. This is just a dream to you, you understand? Goodnight.' She slept off.

I tried to wake her up for the next few minutes. She pretended to be asleep. I couldn't succeed. After a few attempts, I found myself in a deep sleep, holding her hand tight.

Chapter 19

Two days later

Whenever I asked Poo about the talk we had that night, she always told me, 'That dream was so stupid, right? We both dreamt the same dream, and you still remember it? I don't remember it properly.' No matter how hard I tried to get things out of her, she remained undiscovered. But I was not the one who would give it away so easily. I never stopped trying. Pradeep seemed to have forgotten me. Not even a single call from him in the past two days. His service may be under roaming, or there might be no network coverage in his area. He never tried to contact me. His cell phone was always switched off or out of reach whenever I called him.

Dad seemed to have changed a lot. He came home every night, and he slept alone! Yesterday when I searched for his porn DVD collection, I couldn't find any. He might have thrown it away. I was disappointed that moment, but I was happy to see him getting good. But also, it scared me a little.

Last time when he tried to change, a disaster happened, and who knows what would happen this time?

Holidays seemed to be so boring. We didn't have any work to do—that too in the absence of Pradeep and in the occasional presence of Poo. Things were so lonely. I was a kind of girl who would love to be pampered. I just loved the attention given to me. I felt so great when people said I was beautiful, but for now, the two persons who used to pamper me seemed to have left me alone.

I made myself look my best and took photos of mine. I spent hours to put special effects to those photos and posted them on Facebook. People said that the photos were nice, and many commented that I was beautiful, cute, glamorous, and all. I was getting all the attention I wanted. After a long time, finally, I got all my Facebook friends back. I gave them the exam as the reason for me not going online all these days. Yet again, Facebook held my hand when all left me. But I never found Amar online. I didn't even want him to. I wanted to be away from him, but things didn't always happen the way we expected them to happen.

'Hello, remember me?' Amar was online.

I knew it was not good to text him. But for now, I just didn't have the intentions of flirting with him. I wanted to make it clear to him that what happened has to be forgotten, so I joined the chat.

'Yeah, I won't forget anyone so easily.'

'Someone wasn't texting me all these days.'

'I was busy with the exams. How are you doing?'

'As usual, life is boring . . .'

'Why are you looking so down? What happened?'

'Nothing, feeling bored of this life. Smritha, that day was unforgettable. You had made that day the most memorable day of my life.'

'Please, Amar. Whatever has happened has happened. I think we shouldn't speak about it again. We can be good friends and nothing more than that.'

'So are you regretting for it?'

'Hmm . . . I can't speak about it now.'

'Yeah, you can. We are not strangers. We know each other so well.'

'That's all imagination.'

'You mean to say we are not close, and you and I are not friends?'

'It's not like that, Amar. I mean, what has happened between us is in the imagination, and reality is different, right?'

'Tell me the truth. You didn't like it that day?'

'No.'

'Then why did you go on with it?'

'I don't have an answer.'

'You should have! Now think about it. There is only one life, Smritha. We both loved it. That's reality, and doing things that we love is life.'

'That might be truth, but please, can we talk something else?'

'Look, don't you trust me? If I was a cheat, then the whole world would have known about that chat by now. It is not just sex pulling me towards you.'

'Then?' I guess things were going out of control.

'Don't ask me . . . Forget it.'

'No, please tell me, Amar . . . Please.'

'I love you.' I was stunned by the message, but it was so good to hear these words from others. I felt great, but I couldn't reply him with anything. I signed out.

Things were getting tight in my life. I had Pradeep, who loved me so much, on one hand. I had Amar, who was so handsome and romantic, on the other hand. Obviously, my first choice was Pradeep but couldn't make the relationship with Amar to go away. It had been so nice with him. I went back online.

'I know you would come back.' Amar posted with loads of smileys.

'Amar, let me tell you a few things. I like you only as a friend. I can't love you, but sure, we can be good friends.'

'I can't live like that, faking to myself.'

'It's not faking . . . Look, our friendship will remain a secret. We will be very close friends, but don't declare me as your lover.'

My whole idea was to use Poo's concept. I could become his friend, and I could change his love to friendship, and finally, I would have Pradeep as my husband, and Amar would remain my friend forever.

'All right. You sure will love me when you become close to me.'

'You will realize that we are better off friends.'

'Then being friends means I can share anything with you right?'

'Yeah, sure.'

'Then it's fine. Smritha, you should spend time with me. You should understand how much I love you, and the only way you can understand it is by being very close to me.'

'All right, as you say, but there is one thing—all this must be a secret. Not even your close friends should know about our relationship.'

'Your wish is my command, my love.'

'You make me blush.' I couldn't stop him as he made me feel better. He sure was making me feel special. It was what I had missed for many days. Pradeep had forgotten to show me this love. Now I was enjoying the pampering, and I signed off after some friendly chat.

Ever since this day, Amar became part of my life. He asked for my number, but I restricted him to the Internet. I started using Facebook on my mobile. Every day I would start the day with his good-morning message and would end it with his goodnight message. Days passed on like this. He always showed me so much love. I would remember Pradeep, but he was not responding to my messages. Neither did he call. Whenever I called him, it was switched off. I was slowly getting addicted to Amar. I wanted to tell this to Poo, but I was scared at how she would take my relationship with him. The only courage I had was that she would understand it as she was almost in the same situation with the Mr X.

Meanwhile, Amar and I were getting closer. We would discuss almost all topics. He became so close in a span of few days. We started speaking even about sex, romance, and love. Every now and then, I reminded him that I was not his love. Finally, after ten days since we started chatting, we decided to meet up. He suggested a place where he could get a lot of privacy to speak with me. I thought of taking him to the place where I had taken Pradeep on his birthday and expected lot of fun, romance, and love on the next day. I knew what I was doing. I was just spending a day with my true friend who loved me so much, and there was nothing wrong about it.

Chapter 20

Next day, 8 a.m.

'Where are you taking me?' Amar had messaged me.

'To a special place. You will love it for sure.'

'Hmm . . . so we will go on my bike. Be near the college by nine thirty, all right?'

'Fine with me, and make sure we only speak today.'

'That depends on you. Make sure you don't tempt me and make those imaginations a reality.'

'Hmm, I will try. So are you taking me on your bike? I always dreamt about this, Amar. Going with you on your bike in high speed. That's what I call life.'

'So planning to start romance on bike itself?'

'Nooo, stop it.'

'Hmm, Pradeep never took you like this?'

'He? Bike? He only sits behind me. He is not that stylish. Now, why are you asking about him? It has been two weeks since he left me and not even a single call from him. And let me remind you, he is just my friend.'

'Yeah, I know.'

'Now tell me, what are you wearing?'

'Keep guessing.'

'Attitude. All right, don't tell me. Let's see whether our outfits match up or not.'

'You remember the joke I told you? I will wear white and come. At least you will match me from inside.'

'Stupid. Bye.'

I was asking myself whether I would be fine with him! I knew Pradeep was not with me now. That idiot had forgotten me, or he might be doing this purposefully. He might want me to go away. For a few days, he was proper with me, so I guess he was ditching me. I was confused. For now, it was Amar who was making me smile, and there was nothing wrong in being happy and doing things which made me happy.

I was wearing a short top, which was baby pink and bit tight fit, and a pencil cut pants. I wanted to look cool and modern with Amar. He was so forward in mind. I wanted to match up with his style.

I made up myself look hot and left my place. My Pinku was ticking around nine.

I took an auto to reach the college as I knew I would go on his bike. I was nearing the college and was just thinking about the things which happened to me in the past two years. Life seemed to be so strange. A stranger became a loved one, and a loved one became a stranger in this journey of life. We never know who is ours and who is not, but I realized that only I could love myself forever—neither could Pradeep nor Poo nor Amar. People love us for a certain amount of time. Whenever love is given, we have to accept and enjoy it. When there is no love from others, we have to love ourselves.

My phone began to ring. It was Pradeep. I was shocked. Last night I had called him but found it to be switched off. I was so happy and took the call immediately.

'Are you mad? Idiot, where have you been? Do you remember that there is someone waiting for you? Couldn't you call me at least once in all these days?' There was huge anxiety in my voice. I didn't know the reason. It might be because I was happy to receive a call from him after a long gap, or it might be because I was scared of getting known about Amar and me.

'Wow, one questions at a time, my love. It's been so long since I heard from you. Can't you be calm and romantic?' He was laughing over phone.

'Romantic? I feel like killing you. Why did you do this to me?' My voice became serious. For a moment, only Pradeep was in my mind.

'Don't you trust me? I didn't leave you. I was just away from you. That's it. Look, today I have entered into some place where I could find network coverage. I will be in Bangalore in three to four hours. You will be waiting to see me, right?' He had so much love in his voice.

'Yeah, I'm dying to. Call me up when you come here. Take a rest today. I will meet you up tomorrow.

You are going to your hostel after coming here, right?' I tried not to mix up the things.

'I'm going nowhere. I want to see you first. I will deal with everything else later on.'

'I wish I could even see you, but . . .'

'But what? Are you busy?'

'No, it's not like that. Actually, today I have to attend a house warming ceremony of Dad's friend,' I lied.

'So finally you started developing love on your father?' he said it sarcastically. I knew he was disappointed. I also wanted to see him, but as he was coming today, I could meet up with Amar and tell him that I was already in love and try to explain to him my situation. He would remain a good friend to me, and I would convince him not to bring up our secret fantasies towards each other to anyone. I knew he would not do anything which would make me bad. I had to confess to Amar and should make him understand my situation.

'I am asking you something!' Pradeep yelled against my silence.

'You know that I don't love my dad. If I get the licence to kill anyone, I would kill him. Actually, I'm going because of his friend. He is a good human being, and he has invited me personally. In fact, I'm already on my way. His daughter and I are friends. She even called me. Pradeep, I also want to see you. It's been weeks. Please wait. Maybe this evening I can see you, please? Understand me,' I pleaded.

'I understand, sweetie. You all right? Hmm, I will freshen up first and then meet you up in the evening, all right?'

'That's my Pradeep. You know what?'

'Hmm . . . That you love me?'

'Idiot . . . Miss you.' I smiled.

'All right then. Keep texting now. Love you, miss you. Bye.' He hung up the call.

My Pinku was ticking, and minutes had passed, but there was no sign of Amar. He might be here any minute, and I should prepare to make this day fun and also get rid of complications. I checked the Net in my mobile to see whether he had left any message for me, and he had.

'I'm very sorry, darling. I'm on an emergency. I have to go somewhere, but sure, I will meet you up in the afternoon. I will leave a message at once about where and how. Please don't mistake me. It's a sort of emergency. Miss you.'

Bloody emergency. Things were not going on my way. I could have met with Pradeep instead and met with Amar some other day. I was struck in the middle of nowhere without my Pleasure. I decided to call up Pradeep and tell him that I would cancel up everything and was coming to see him. He would be happy, thinking that I was sacrificing so much to him.

My cell phone again began to ring. It was Poo this time. Oh god! What was up with her now? I received it.

'Smritha, I need your help.' She was scared.

'Help? Tell me what it is.' I was tense.

'Look, it's been so long since he and I met. He badly wants to meet, it seems, but I can't meet out with him alone. Can you come along? You will also get to know about him, please?' Things were getting tighter now. So I could meet with Poo now, then later afternoon I could meet with Amar, then in the evening, I would meet up with Pradeep, and I would call it a day. I hoped I wouldn't mess up with time.

'All right, what time?' I was not very much excited about that guy whom she loved, but since every time Pradeep and I went out, she had helped me out, it was now my job, I guess.

'Thank you . . . Maybe in an hour? You suggest the place.' She seemed happy.

'Hmm . . . Look, I'm already out of my house, so make it as early as possible. Come by half an hour near the college. We will go to that ice-cream parlour. Call him there, okay?' I made things clear for her.

'So early? Hmm, all right. I will be as early as I can.' She hung up the call.

I started to walk on the pathway alone. I could see the windows of my classrooms from the road. I used to sit and sleep near the windows in class. Those were beautiful memories. For a second, my entire last two years came in front of me. I could not believe all that had happened in the past few years. I had gradually changed so much.

As I walked on the road, watching the college, my mind started searching for the views inside—benches, classrooms, blackboards, irritating yet funny teachers, textbooks, chemistry lab, test tubes, acids and bases, funny colour-changing chemicals, biology lab, microscope, slides, microorganism, Newton's laws, optical experiments in physics lab, caring and helpful lab attendees. I began to reminisce our secret mobile messaging in the classrooms, Poo pinching me now and then and making a face, me trying to turn at Pradeep and noticing that he was already looking at me and smiling.

Everything flashed in front of me in the form of slides. Unknowingly, a few drops of tears rolled down my cheeks. 'I will miss you,' I said to my college. It was a place where I spent most of my life for two years. No matter how much I used to get mad with this college, now I was missing it. I checked out Pinku. She told me it was a long way for Poo to come. I decided to enter the college and have a glance. I was in the mood to recall everything. I entered the gate with hesitation. The place, which meant nothing to me before, meant so special all of a sudden. My eyes were wet. I passed across the parking place, the place where Poo used to get me breakfast so many times, the place where we used to sit and chat for hours together. My hand brushed the two-wheelers of my teachers.

'Now I can't park my Pleasure here,' I said to myself and moved on. My physics teacher came near me. I greeted him. He smiled and patted me on my shoulders. It seemed to convey a lot. I sure would miss all of my teachers. Every corner of the college began to be so special. I sat near the corridor and closed my eyes, wishing to remember more. I tried to recall the memories of my first day there. I came into the college, knowing no one except Poo. That day, we both entered with hesitation. The memories brought a small smile.

I tried to remember what I studied. When it came to physics, I learned everything from period to frequency, from velocity to wavelength, from angular frequency to wave number. I began to recall path difference, phase difference, waves, super position, vectors, scalars, Newton's formulae, Doppler effect, reflection, refraction, radiation, resonance, polarization, Coulomb's law, electric potential, electric flux, electric field, capacitors, current density, resistance, colour code, tolerance, series connection, parallel connection, thermistor, Kirchhoff's laws, wheatstone network, Biot–Savart law, magnetic induction, tangent galvanometer, modern physics, photo electric effect, Einstein's photoelectric equation, electrons, photons, radioactive decay, atom, half-life of uranium, viscosities, gas laws, Stoke's law, thermal conductivity, Planck's radiation law, optics, focal length, refractive index, critical angle, dispersion, lens equation, logical gates, constants (like alpha, beta, gamma). The whole physics flashed in front of me in a fraction of a second. I wish I could recall so much in the exam.

Now I went back to recall chemistry. Boyle's law, Charles's law, kinetic theory of glasses, stoichiometry, mole, Avogadro number, atomic weight, acids, bases, oxidizing agents, reducing agents, normality, modality, and morality, volumetric analysis, vapour density, periodic table, chemical bonding, ionic bond, covalent bond, hydrogen bond, methane, ethylene, acetylene, benzene, physical chemistry, crystal structure, chemical equation—oh god, I can't remember more. Someone patted me on my shoulder.

'Feeling bad to leave the college?' a teacher said. It was my language teacher.

'Very much, ma'am.' I looked at her.

'The doors of the college are always open for you. You can come anytime and meet with us.' She smiled and walked away.

I checked out Pinku. She was ticking fast but still no sign of Poo. Even after finishing the exams, I was feeling so scared to use my mobile in campus. I went to the restroom and called up Poo. She was almost near the college. Now it was time to leave the campus. I promised myself that I would come back once again to recall mathematics (from partial fractions to integration) and biology (from species classification to human reproduction). In fact, I needed not to remember human reproduction as I know it by heart! Moreover, a lot of revision had been given by Amar. The thoughts made me smile at myself and walked out of the college.

'Why didn't you bring your vehicle?' Poo started. She was a yard away, walking towards me.

'That's a long story. I will tell you later. Someone is all set to meet the love of her life?' I glanced at her from top to bottom and winked.

'Smritha, you will never learn! He is not my love. I'm just meeting him because he was missing me very much.' She folded her arms and started staring at me.

'So in the future you might even marry him, saying that he will miss you.' I giggled, and we walked together to the coffee shop. Poo went serious about my words.

'Why are you taking those words seriously? All right, you both are friends. Are you happy now?' I said.

'No . . .' She didn't even look at me.

'Then what else can I say?' I raised my eyebrows.

'I liked to be teased with him.' She laughed. We both poked each other and chatted about the past and tried to sort out the differences.

'Where are you, Romeo? I can't wait more,' I said.

'Hmm, he will come soon.' She smiled.

'Then at least tell me an incident where he impressed you.' I ordered a cold coffee.

'Actually, it's not like getting impressed or something like that. I liked the way he proposed to me, but I didn't accept it.' She was blushing.

'You want me to trust your last sentence? All right, I will! Now tell me about that proposal thing.'

She was expressive with her eyes. 'It was late at night and was raining heavily. I was peeping out through the window, and he called me over the phone. In fact, he was showing huge amount of care already by that time. I just asked him why he was getting attached to me so much, and he asked me back why I was close to him and why I was not treating him in the way I treat other boys. I had no answer. Silence reigned. Then he explained the theory of heat transfer.' She laughed.

'Heat transfer? What are you talking about?' I was shocked.

'Yeah. It's his theory! Actually, he explained to me a few things. Now think that you are me and I'm him, and I will tell it to you the way he told me.' She came close to me.

'You are him? All right.' I laughed aloud, and she turned aside. After a little pleading, she began to speak.

'You know how heat transfer takes place? It's by conduction, convection, and radiation. In this theory, I'm relating love to heat! Long back when you passed by me, I was blessed by the pleasure of experiencing your touch accidently. You had a huge amount of love in the form of matter inside you. According to $E = mc^2$, matter and energy are interconvertible. So matter got converted into energy, and it was transmitted to me by conduction. It now spread all over my blood by convection and now finally, my body is filled with such heat energy, and I cannot convert it into matter. Hence, I'm radiating it back to you in the form of care!' she said.

'Wow! He sounds interesting—a beautiful mixture of science and love.' He reminded me of Pradeep.

'And I asked him what I was supposed to do. He gave me two options. I can either become a moon and reflect back the radiation or a black body and absorb all his radiation which comes to me in the form of love.' She smiled.

'And you became a moon and loved him back?' I poked her.

'No, I became a black body! I just absorbed huge amount of love from him. I never gave him anything.' She turned serious.

'Why?' I said.

'Because I'm a black body, and a black body can only absorb. It won't radiate.' She turned more serious.

'You are an emotional fool, Poo. He seems to love you very much. Don't lose him,' I said.

'In fact, I don't want to lose him too, and I also know I can't get a better man than him. But all that happens only in movies, Smritha. Dad might even kill him. Moreover, none will be happy except us. Tell me, won't I be selfish if I marry this guy, hurting the entire family? My dad trusts me so much. He would collapse to death if I disobey him.' Her eyes were turning red.

'Now, don't cry. Let's live in the present. We will think about it in the future. When he comes, he would not like to see your tears.' I moved my arm over her shoulder.

'Once, Dad told me that he had a dream, watching me run out of the door. He was making fun of the dream. I realized that deep inside him he has that fear. I should not hurt his emotions. And you know what that idiot told me when I told him about this serious matter? He told me that we should always make our parents' dream come true.' I could see tears in her eyes as well as a smile on her lips.

I checked my Pinku. She was ticking fast. I didn't want to mess up with my first meet-up with Amar.

'In fact, there is another reason to call you. Let him come. Let's talk together,' she said.

It was turning to be afternoon. I was getting late. I thought going online to see his status, but before I could realize what happened, Amar was sitting in front of me! I looked at him and then at Poo. Both looked tense. She might be wondering what this guy was doing here, and I didn't know how to react. Before I could speak something, Poo broke the silence.

'This is the guy! You know him, right?' I was stunned to the silence. I looked at him. He introduced himself as a new person to me. This guy was a huge flirt. He had spent nights talking to me over the Internet about love, lust, and sex, and now he was playing a game with my lovely friend. And he was sitting in front of me without fear.

'So this is the second time we meet, and in both times, I have given you surprises, right?' Amar spoke up.

'You have told me many times that you have chatted with him, but he always used to tell me that it was not him. I thought of asking you before, but I couldn't let you know about our friendship, so I kept quiet,' she said.

'That is not true, Poo. Don't believe him. I think he played in both of our lives.' All three faces became serious.

'Played with you? You said that you just had a friendly chat with him,' she fired back immediately.

'Then that day why did you follow me? Why did you come to me in the rain?' I looked straight towards Amar.

'I didn't follow you! Poo and I had a small fight the previous night of that day. She was having health problems also, and she had consumed sleeping pills to get some sleep. I had been near her house to check her out. She never picked my call. I saw you coming out of her house, so I approached you to know about her condition. Remember? I had asked about her that day.' He sounded convincing.

'And why did you always stare at me in the college? Why did you always roam around me in bike?' I wanted answer to my every question.

'Smritha, remember, you were not alone. Poo was always with you. In fact, I was seeing her. You have misunderstood me,' he said.

'Then you never chatted with me? You didn't propose to me? Is that not you whom I chatted all these days and nights? I was in a state of confusion.

'Propose? What are you saying, Smritha? You didn't tell me about all these. I didn't know this would go this serious. I just thought someone pranked you in his name. Every time you spoke about your chat with him, I confirmed from him that it was not him. Someone had created a profile in his name and has played with your emotions.' Poo was damn serious and confident about him now.

'Yeah, someone played with my emotions,' I said.

'No, you played with my emotions.' A familiar voice from a boy who was seated behind our seats made the three of us look at him. He turned towards us. It was Pradeep. For a moment, all turned shocked. I had planned to meet all three of you today but not together—that too not like this! Pradeep walked into our table and sat down right in front of me.

'Smritha, it was me who was chatting with you all these days in his name. I'm sorry for that, Amar. Poo, she is not the way she actually looks now. There is a cruel mind behind this innocent face.' He was pointing his finger straight to my face.

'What's all these, Pradeep? You don't trust her? It's cheap to check on a love like this. Moreover, what's wrong in making friends with others?' Poo stood up for me.

'Is it not wrong to talk about sex with friends? Is it not wrong to wish someone else on bed other than me? Is it not wrong to degrade me in her sex fantasy? Is it not wrong to lie to me and plan to spend a romantic day with him?' Pradeep sure looked scary for the first time. Poo looked stunned. Amar looked confused, having no idea about what was happening.

'It can't be you,' I whispered.

'It is,' he commanded.

'Many times you were not online when I was chatting. I remember you being over the phone when I was chatting in the cyber cafe,' I whispered again.

'It was my roommate. He actually planned to prank you at the beginning. He was shocked by your positive response. Later on, he showed me the truth, and in the past few months, all the sex chat of yours was with me. You are a bitch.' He was about to slap me. I went crying in Poo's arms.

'Pradeep, all that chat was with you only, and moreover, it was just a chat over the Net. She was not involved directly, right? Still, she is pure,' Poo said, wiping my tears.

'Today she was all set to be involved, Poo. That's why she is wearing that outfit, to tempt her fantasy. Poo, trust me, if by chance she had been raped by someone, I would have still accepted her, but what she did is not forgivable. She does not know what love is. She is just thinking about her own pleasure at the moment. She doesn't damn think about others.' His finger pointed at me, and he was scolding me hard.

'Then why did you leave me alone? I was so lonely.' I spoke a bit stronger now.

'So? You found a substitute? You are only concerned about yourself. Could you not wait for me? You just want a man to be with you. It does not matter who it is. It can be Pradeep or Amar or someone else. Who knows? I hate you, Smritha. I hate you. You have lost me. You will never get me back. Never try to contact me again. You will find a new sex partner online. Enjoy your life.' He split up with me and walked out straight away. I could see all my hopes walk away with him. Amar also moved out without a word, and I was left alone with Poo on her shoulders.

I burst out into tears. Yes, I was bad. I was a bitch. I should not have done all these. I destroyed my own life. I was only concerned about my pleasure. But I was still a human being. I wished to get a chance to prove myself. Poo and I walked out of the place together.

'I knew you were fun-loving but never expected you to be this cheap,' Poo whispered.

'You also hate me?' I cried harder.

'I'm ashamed of you, Smritha.' She walked away and soon went out of sight, catching an autorickshaw.

I looked around. I was all alone now. No Pradeep, no Poo, and no Mom. I started recalling everything and regretting every mistake and walked towards home, shedding tears all along.

Chapter 21

Same day, 10 p.m.

My eyes were dry. It no longer had tears to shed. I guess the last time I cried this much was when I lost my mom. I knew no loved one would stay with me for long—first mother and now Pradeep. Even Poo was unhappy with me. No one would ever forgive me. I never expected things to happen this way. Every little thing turned out to be against me, but I couldn't blame anyone other than myself for my present situation. I just had Dad as someone for me, but I didn't want him. I wanted Pradeep, but he was no longer my Pradeep.

This was one of the worst days of my life. It made me experience so many feelings. Most of them were what I never wanted to experience again. I guess my nightmares could come true today. I might lead towards Mom. I had no one for me. I hated myself. I was such a cheat. I ruined my own life. I didn't do well in the exams also. Now education couldn't hold my hands, and I couldn't expect Pradeep to hold it again.

I looked around my room. This place knew all about me, all my dirty secrets. These walls knew how much I had struggled. These pillows were soaked in my tears. My hands brushed over the pillow. It was still wet. Most of my life I found it to be wet.

I began to see no future. I moved on to the kitchen to get some water. I was on the same dress which I had worn in the morning. I was feeling uncomfortable with the tight top. I was not in the mood to change. I found the water in the fridge. I was hungry but was not in the mood to eat. I thought I must die, rejecting food daily. I checked out Pinku. She was showing eleven. I went to check out Dad. He was sleeping in his room. I walked back slowly to the kitchen. There was something glittering in the dark—it was the sharp edge of the knife. Yes, it was a dream come true to me—a nightmare come true, to be accurate. I took the knife and moved on to the room.

I saw a cute smile on Mom's face in a photo. I switched on the night light. The room became pale blue due to the colour of the night light. I looked into the mirror and tried to imitate Mom's smile. I couldn't copy it. Mine was fake, while hers was genuine.

My mother wouldn't forgive me for my behaviour. I knew she would be ashamed to have a daughter like me. I was not only a cheat but also an idiot. I could not find the truth myself. I assumed myself to be brilliant, but Pradeep showed me how foolish I really was.

I took the knife in my hand; the sharp edge looked beautiful. I had seen this knife more than 100 times by this time, but now, it seemed to be lovable. It was my friend now, a friend who would show me the path away from this world, a friend who would send me to my mother. I placed the edge of the knife near the nerve on my forearm. The moment had come. I was going away far into the place where no one could ever find me. I remembered everyone at this moment.

'Mom, I'm sorry. Dad, at least live a good life from now on. Poo, I will be missing you. Pradeep, I still love you. If possible, all of you, forgive me,' I said to myself.

This moment was so cruel. I removed the knife from there and pierced the sharp tip of the knife into my fingertip. I went in front of the mirror. Blood was oozing out from my finger. I wrote my death note on the mirror.

'Everyone, please forgive me. I myself take the responsibility of my death.' It was painful. The blood was not sticking on the mirror. I pressed on to get more blood. It hurt. It seemed like I was in hell already. I traced the words. Now it was legible. I never knew I would use my finger as a pen and blood as the ink.

Now it was time to cut my nerves. It might be an easy death, a painless death. For a girl who lost everyone, pain should be felt, at least to reduce the guilt. I made the sharp edge of the knife make its mark on my left wrist. It started bleeding. Later on, my skin separated off by the sharp cut. I began to scream; I was in pain. The blanket was full of blood now. The pillow which had seen only tears was now experiencing my blood too. Things were getting too painful. I must die now.

I sat down on my study chair. Soon my nerve was cut. I laid my hand on the table, watching my blood flowing out of my nerves. Blood was spreading all over the table. It was all over now. The only thing I could do was to wait for my death. I closed my eyes. The cuts were painful; I opened my eyes slowly to check the amount of blood flowing out of my nerves. Nothing seemed to be clear. All I could see was a blurred red colour. Things slowly went out of my control. I was getting closer and closer to death with every second my Pinku was ticking.

Chapter 22

Date: unknown
Time: unknown

I could not open my eyes but tried to open them slowly. I thought something pierced into my right hand. I checked out my left hand. It was wrapped with a white bandage. The piercing thing on my right hand was the glucose drip.I was lying down in the hospital, having no clue after I went unconscious. I didn't know how many days I had been in the hospital. Everything seemed to have happened long back. I didn't even know whether it was morning or night. I tried to call someone, but I could not speak. Finally, when I called for help, no one seemed to respond.

It was a long wait. I kept on looking at the lights. There were no windows. Air conditioning was cold, and I could not see any human activities for hours together. I thought Pinku could help me to know the time, but she was not in my hand. The last time I remember seeing her was when I was bleeding.

My body seemed to be bit responding now. I tried to step down. A nurse came in.

'What are you trying to do? Sleep. Don't get up.' She was wearing a completely white dress. I could not answer her. I just followed her words.

'Look. Don't do anything stupid until I come back. Wait patiently. I will call the doctor and your dad. You girls don't even know the seriousness of life.' She was walking out of the room, murmuring something. I sure knew that it was something against me.

The next few minutes were a hopeless wait for nothing. Finally, Dad and the doctor entered into the room.

'Thank you, Doctor. You saved my daughter—both from death and the police.' Dad was hugging him. There were tears in his eyes. I wondered how he could have such an emotion for me in his eyes. I didn't see anything like this when Mom died.

'That's nothing. It's the least I can do for our friendship.' The doctor began to wipe his specs with some cloth. I kept my silence. Now the question the whole world would ask me was *why*! I didn't have the answer. Even if I had, I couldn't tell this to the world. I was confused. At present, I felt happy to be still breathing but couldn't understand why.

The doctor soon left the place after inspecting me for the next ten minutes. Dad pulled the chair near me. It was Dad and I alone now in this room. He broke the silence.

'I won't ask you why you did something like this. I know you would have a strong reason for it, and I may be also one of the reasons for it. All I want is to talk to you for two minutes and tell you why you should not do this again.' I saw a face which was tired of emotions. He had a charm in his face. He was waiting to tell me something.

'You need no permission to speak to your daughter.' I looked away from him.

'All right, how are you feeling now?' His hand moved over my forehead. I guess this was the first time I was experiencing Dad's love.

'Better, but . . . I don't know. I just wanted to say sorry. I should not have tried to kill myself, but since I have done it, I should not have survived.' I closed my eyes.

'I thought I should not ask, but I feel like wanting to know it now. Share it with me, I can help. What made you do this? Explain.'

'Explain? Hmm, do you know Hitler? Adolf Hitler from Germany? Who once ruled the world? He said we should not lose anything in life, and if we lose, we should not be alive to explain our defeat,' I said.

'So what did you lose? Who defeated you?' He was charging in.

'It does not matter. You will never know about it.'

'Look, Smritha, I don't know what's wrong with you, but let me tell you something which I came to know recently. It's something which I should not share with you. It's something which I'm ashamed of, but still I want you to know about it because I don't want you to do something which your mother also did.' He took a deep breath.

'Mom? What did she do? All her life she struggled to make you happy. That's the only thing she ever did.'

'I agree with you. She is a great woman. She has sacrificed something which any other woman can't do for her husband. I never knew about her sacrifice till a few weeks back. Before that, I want to tell you the bitter truth.' He was looking down.

'The bitter truth? What it is? I hate you, Dad. You were so cruel. You didn't even cry for losing such a loving wife. I hate you.'

'Your mother's death was not accidental. It was intentional. She killed herself.' His emotions burst out. He started crying. I was shocked at the second I heard him. I sat down in shock.

'What? Mom committed suicide? Why? Things were getting on for her. You had taken her so far to finally prove that you love her. She was happy the last time I saw her. I don't believe you. Tell me what actually happened!'

His head was still down. I could hear him sobbing. 'There are so many things which you don't know, Smritha. I don't know whether it's right to tell you, but all I want is for you to understand the truth and promise me that you won't kill yourself like my wife did.'

'Please, let me know.' I slowly grew emotional.

'I will tell you what happened on that day of your mom's death, but before that, you should read this.' He took a file from his bag and put it on my bed.

'What's this?'

You know, Smritha, your mom was a reserved kind of woman. I found that gem in Mangalore long back and married her, but when I finally realized that it was a gem, I had lost it! She never used to share anything with anyone, and the only thing she trusted and shared with was her diary. This file, you see, it's not an ordinary file. I hand-picked the pages from her diary to make you realize what actually happened to her. It contains her handwritten manuscript which she had written from past twenty-five years back. It has her entire life story. I want you to read it. I will talk to you later. Once you get better, I will give you all her dairies. You can read them all. But these sheets which I'm giving you are very precious. Take care of them. I will come back tonight. We will speak about it.' He stood up. His head never looked straight.

'But, Dad . . .' I paused.

'I love you, Smritha. Your dad is not as bad as you think. You will understand me even more once you read it.' He touched my cheeks and walked away.

Things began to confuse me. I knew Mom was not happy with Dad. But later on he was changed, so Mom was happy. Why would she commit suicide? Things began to poke into my head. I saw the file next to me. It was a big leather-bound file. I took it with my left hand as my right hand was not movable. I put it on my lap and opened it. Dad had divided the sheets into stages. He had put his letter also. It read:

> Smritha, this is your mother's deepest secret. I made sure to arrange them in order for you. This will make you understand your parents and, indeed, your life also. Even after reading this, please accept me as your father.
>
> Dad

I turned the first sheet. It was the first stage.

Stage 1

> It's before I met your mother. She was an innocent girl from Mangalore. This will tell you all the dreams which she had dreamt before marrying me.

21 May 1985

> Hello, Diary. I turned eighteen years today, so wish me a very happy birthday. I'm already of legal age. Mom cannot hit me, nor can dad control me. I'm so happy. Diary, in fact, they are busy searching a guy for me. I know I'm not

yet prepared for marriage, but I'm happy because both Mom and Dad will be happy. They would be relieved when I get married, so I also agreed.

Today Mom had prepared superb meals. I wish you also had a digestive system. And guess what, it was drizzling today. I visited three temples. You know, Lord Banashankari was looking superb. Today the decoration to her was so good. I had goosebumps seeing her. I prayed her to make Mom and Dad happy. And nothing much happened. I stayed at home the rest of the day. Tomorrow when I go to the college, I will give some sweets to my friends. All right then, let me get some sleep. Will see you tomorrow, bye and miss you.

23 May 1985

Hello, Diary . . . Mom, Dad, and I have been to dinner outside, so I came and slept off as I was tired. Yesterday my dad asked me how my husband should be. You know how much I blushed? Look, I remained pure for this unknown guy all these years. I never fell in love as I love my parents. And finally, I'm given licence to love. I'm feeling shy.

Yesterday was normal. Nothing much special to tell except that dinner. I kept a huge list of demands for my hero. Dad was shocked to see my expectation. I told Dad that he should be handsome, talented, fair, and good-looking. He should have the best caring nature (only to me). He should be understanding, and he should keep quiet when I'm angry. And he should know cooking and all. Dad was laughing so much, I'm so lucky to get such great parents. They are like my friends. They love me so much. I thought of telling my friends about my arranged marriage, but I decided not to say anything unless it's final.

Granny came over from her home town. She must be so lonely in her home town. After Grandpa passed away, she stopped sharing things with anyone. I wish I would not outlive my unknown hero. I should die a few minutes before he dies. You know why? I will love him so much, just like the way Mom loves Dad, and I cannot bear to see him dead. He will also love me very much. He can't take my death, so he will die a few seconds after I die, and we will go to heaven together. I want to love him so much, and I want him to love me more than I love him. And this is my final year of studying. I won't be pursuing a degree. That's what Dad said, Diary. I want to study more, but it's okay if I don't. I'm so lucky that he made me study this long. All my school friends dropped off their studies after school. I will get back to you tomorrow.

28 May 1985

Hello, Today Granny made me wear a sari. Seriously speaking, I was completely shy. I was never used to expose the sides of the waist to the sun! Granny told me that I will get used to it in the future, it seems. Yeah . . . let me tell you how I looked. I was wearing a maroon-and-purple sari. The flare was beautiful at the front. Granny only made me wear a back-cut blouse. I was wearing jasmine flowers on my hair. And yeah, there was a red rose at the centre of the jasmine. Long earrings . . . I'm feeling shy to let you know everything.

Can you guess why I had worn sari? A guy had come to see me. He is a businessman in Bangalore, it seems. I know it will be difficult for a Mangalore girl to settle in Bangalore. But his family is very good, it seems. Dad was so happy. But I did not see the guy properly. I could not lift my head. I was shy. Dad and Mom said he is handsome. Since they like him so much, that obviously means he is good-looking. Anyway, they know what's best for me, right?

This is the first guy who came to see me with a marriage proposal, and it seems like their minds are fixed to have him as my husband. But I'm worried. If I get married to this guy, it would be a whole new world to me. New city, new culture, new people. I don't know how I could manage. Moreover, how can I leave Dad? If I don't remind him, he might always forget to take BP tablets. I'm scared. I can't go away from my parents. Tell me, why do girls have to leave their loved ones behind and go? Why can't boys live in the girl's house? I know it sounds funny, but girls are always given the pain. It's the gift from God. Take care, Diary. Goodnight.

31 May 1985

Hello, Diary. Talks about marriage have increased. Everyone is talking about it. I think it will be difficult for Dad to do this marriage. The boy's side is very rich, it seems, so Mom was telling me it's very difficult to fulfil all their expectations. Dad is worried. He is trying to sell some property, it seems. In fact, I don't want heaven in exchange with my dad's tears. But they will be happy when I settle with this guy, so I'm keeping quiet. This is the dark side of my marriage.

I also want to tell you about the bright side. Dad had been to their place yesterday, and he returned today. He says it's quite far, but they seem to be rich. They have their own house in Bangalore. It seems a beautiful city. Looks like I will land up in a modern world. Just imagine my husband and me going for a jog early morning in the mist, just like in movies. It will be superb. And we both drink coffee in a chilly morning, sharing a single cup! It's romantic, right?

I know what you are thinking. How come a decent girl changed so fast! Okay now, tell me, that's my husband and I have the rights.

Things seem to be changing in my mind. I wondered how I changed like this. I have so many new desires. Actually, Mom and Dad were telling that my future husband will be coming here by next week. And he will be staying here with his cousins. For two days. Hmm, actually, they know that he is coming here to check out on us, but they pretend that he is coming to see me. Tell me, he will be nice, right? All my dreams will come true, right? Mom and Dad will be happy, right? I'm scared. Goodnight.

3 June 1985

Hello, Diary. Wow, I'm so excited. He is like a prince. He came to our home early morning. Dad had been to the railway station to pick him up. He is so cute. You will definitely fall in love with him. I did not see him properly last time, but now finally, I see him. I spoke to him, but he was not friendly. I felt a bit disappointed. He was always serious. He didn't speak much and always kept staring down. I guess he is shy! He is a true man. My man. Finally, I could love someone, and I have got the best. I'm so happy.

Today we took him to the temple. There, I alone came near Kalyani. The water was peaceful. I was just touching the surface of the water, creating waves, and playing. When I turned back, he was staring at me, laughing at my childish act. I felt so shy. I just ran to Mom.

Actually, I don't know why I felt so shy and just ran to Mom when I felt that he was staring at me. In fact, I want him to stare at me. He will be so serious, but he will have that small smile just for me. Just in one day, how come this stupid girl can judge a guy, right? Hmmm . . . in fact, I fell in love with him! And yeah, now mine is a love marriage.

When my friends got committed, they had challenged me that I won't get good guy if I trust my parents. But Dad made them all to lose. He found me a gem. The people who scolded me when I rejected the guys who proposed to me would realize that I did the right thing now. All will be jealous seeing my lovely husband. I know he is not yet my husband, but soon he will be. Actually, he asked me about my likes and dislikes. He told me he will take good care of me. Whenever we get a chance to talk privately, Mom would hide away and would peek to see us. She looks funny! She is so curious about us. All right, Diary, time to sleep. Goodnight.

4 June 1985

Hi, I had never blushed this much before. Finally, my wedding date is fixed. It's 1 July, twenty-six days to go. Dad had consulted priests, and he also agreed with the dates. Wedding will be done in Mangalore only. Thank God. I was so worried about it. If it were in Bangalore, it means I couldn't call all my friends. Now I can call everyone and shout aloud, 'My hubby is the strongest.'

Actually, I was measuring our height difference without his knowledge. I will come exactly till his chest. Every time I hug him, I will listen to his heart beating for me. It is so romantic, right?

In fact, the only thing I'm upset about is that Dad has promised a huge amount of dowry along with me. He is struggling a lot. Hopefully, everything goes well. I have a lot of work to do nowadays. I have to go to shopping. I have to meet my friends and invite them to my wedding, so I might not come to write you daily. Goodnight.

Stage 2

Your mother was brought to Bangalore by me. She saw the real side of me. Her dreams were so colourful. I made her wash all those colours with her tears, but still she stood strong and never stopped loving me. She begged for love which I never had. Read on.

5 July 1985

Hello, Diary . . . I could not meet you all these days. I'm sorry. Actually, I had lost you. Somehow, I managed to put you in my bag before I left Mangalore. Oh yeah, now you are also in Bangalore. It's such a beautiful place. This house is so beautiful. My husband, my mother-in-law, and I—this is my new family. But for now, everyone is there, from Dad to my distant relatives. I'm feeling shy to tell you something. Tomorrow night will be our first night together, it seems. In fact, the whole world is busy in educating me about this, from my mother to my cousins. They all try to tell me so many things. That too as if I don't know anything!

I'm scared. I don't know what will happen tomorrow night. I guess I might not come to you tomorrow. I mean to say, he won't let me out of his arms. Ha ha! I will share with you moments of our marriage some other day. It's a promise. Goodnight.

6 July 1985

Diary, I can't stop crying. In fact, I'm sitting in the bathroom and writing to you. I had told you that I might not come to you today, but when everyone left me alone, I can only come to you. You are the only one who never pushed me out of your heart.

Today was supposed to be my first night, but it turned out to be the worst day of my life. It scares me, thinking about the upcoming worst nights in the future.

I was sent inside with loads of lessons. I expected huge amount of pampering from him, but what I got was only tears. I entered the room and was just about to sit on the bed when he scolded me that I should not even touch his bed. It has been brought for Gagana, it seems. I don't know who this girl is. But today I realized that he doesn't love me. He has another girl in his life. They both are in love for the past three years, it seems. I don't deserve to be on his bed, it seems. I can't stop these tears. He married me only for the sake of his mother. He told that he will divorce me and get married to Gagana after a year, and he won't touch me, it seems. He wants to remain pure for his love. What mistake have I done? If he loves her, then why should he marry me? I'm left with tears. I feel like running out and creating a scene, but I can't imagine how Dad and Mom would feel. Dad has spent so much of money for my marriage, and it is worth nothing. I tried to scare him that I will complain to his mother, but he said that she knows everything. That lady brought me to correct his son's life, but she hid everything. She used my parents and me. She has sacrificed my life for her greed. I don't know what Dad would feel if he comes to know about it. It's the end of my life. All my dreams are burnt to ashes. I want to die. Seriously, I want to die.

7 July 1985

My only trustworthy friend, all are cheats here. All are using me here. I went and spoke all about this to my mother-in-law. She scolded me. She was complaining that I don't have the potential to pull him towards me. Tell me. Am I a dog? Am I a bitch? All I wanted yesterday was love, not sex. This lady is telling me that once I sleep with him, then everything will be normal. I hate it. This guy might have slept with Gagana. Who knows? I feel disgusted. I can't accept him as my husband, but still I love him, Diary. He is the first and only one whom I have loved till now. I have dreamt thousands of dreams with him. I want his love. I want his love.

I wanted to hide this from Dad and Mom. But guess what, they already knew about it! My mother-in-law told them that her son was in love with another girl, but she said he will be normal after marriage, so they took the whole risk of marrying me to him. It hurts. Was I troubling them? Somehow they managed to kick me out of their house. They showed the whole world that they love me by doing the marriage so grand. But what have they done? They don't love me. They are also cheaters.

Now I don't know where to go. I don't even have any friend other than you. I'm disgusted with my dad for the first time in my life. He just holds the pride of marrying me to a guy from this huge city, but I'm bound to suffer here. My husband doesn't even look at me. He washes his hands if he touches me accidently. Diary, tell me, should a girl like me still be alive in this world?

Today Mom and Dad left for Mangalore. They just advised me to adjust to the situation and promised that everything will be better soon, but I know it will never be. You know what happened this morning? He accidently saw my face first. He spat and took that girl's photo, which was under the pillow. He kissed it and looked at it and then said that now he got purified. I want that love, Diary. I want his love. I don't want to share it with anyone on this planet. He is mine, right? He is my husband. When will he understand? I don't know how to fight. I'm crying inside and sharing this only with you. I'm alone here, Diary. I'm scared. Please hug me as I sleep.

3 August 1985

Dear Diary, look at my fate. He is in huge pain today. He says his day was the worst as I showed him my disgusting face when he went out. Today he has fought with his lover, and he is blaming me. That girl doubts about our relationship, it seems. I should talk to her and tell her about the purity of my husband. Is it not funny? Can any girl endure living a life like mine? Sometimes I wonder whether I'm his wife or a maid-cum-nurse who takes care of their house.

All have their problems. All have their pains. Dad is regretful and feeling the pain for spoiling my life. Mom is feeling the pain of losing everything to no use. My mother-in-law is feeling the pain of losing her son. And my husband is feeling the pain of staying away from his love. All are lost in their pains. No one has the time to think about what I feel. No one asks me about my pain. Why? No one loves me?

No more tears are left. My eyes are dry. They can't cry more. They had enough, but I have the courage. I can face the world, but I need him along. I still love him. Tell me, he will accept me soon, right? You are the only one for my support, but what can you do? You can perhaps wipe my tears, but you can't get him to me. These creatures can't do that at least. I will sleep now. I have to work like an ass in the morning. Goodnight, Diary.

18 November 1985

Hello, Diary. I can't take the torture any more. These people are so cheap. That day I guess I did wrong by making my mother-in-law believe that I'm gaining control over him. She is asking me for happy news. She wants a baby boy, and she wants it as soon as possible. Tell me, when I'm not touched even once, how can I get a baby? I can't tell the truth to all. I feel so ashamed. People might think badly about me, so I don't want to share. It's just been a few months since I got married, and she is torturing me like this. I don't know what she will do if a year passes by.

In fact, I don't have hopes that he will stay with me. Any time he may go with Gagana. Every night when he comes late, I feel so scared. Some night he might not come and I might not see him ever again after that. Hope that day won't come. It won't come right?

I have written a letter to Mom yesterday. I told her I'm happy. I know I lied. But for my Dad, Mom and Granny, I had to lie. At least they will be happy. In fact, all my time here I spend thinking about them. I'm so unlucky.

Last night I heard him talking in his sleep, and it seemed like he was scolding Gagana. He was telling her not to leave him alone. It was not so clear, but all I could understand from his murmuring was that he might have fought with her. In fact, I felt so happy. I hope they would fight like this daily and one day they would break up and never unite again. I hope such a day comes soon. Then at least he might realize my love. I pray to God that at least he will realize my love.

Stage 3

It was almost a year after our marriage. Gagana did never understand me. She was thinking that I was just using her. She wanted me to get divorced soon. She wanted me to talk to her parents and marry her, but there was a sudden disaster in my life. I would love to tell you, but your mother will tell you better. Read it in her own words. Read on.

18 May 1986

Hello, Diary. Finally, some good news. Yesterday I was so scared. I had told you that he didn't come back home, right? You know where he had been? Actually, he was in his friend's place. Luckily, that friend is not Gagana. His name is Samuel. He stays nearby our house. He was home today morning. He was narrating what actually happened and promised me that he will bring my husband back home soon.

Day before yesterday, both Samuel and he had been to a movie, it seems. There they found Gagana in a compromising position with another guy! Seeing this, he got ferocious. Samuel stopped him from creating a scene there. On the same day, she met with my husband without knowing that her secrets are no more a secret, and they fought about it. She slapped him and said that she also wants another man as he is having me. Finally, he slapped her back, and now he is in Samuel's house, regretting for his mistakes. He was crying that he remained pure just for Gagana and she ditched him.

Samuel narrated this entire story to my mother-in-law and me. Now the new hopes are arising. I guess I will be loved soon. The love that I mean is not sex. It's what I wanted in the form of care and concern. Now no one is between him and me. He has started to hate her, so he might come to me. Things will be better for me. I'm so happy, Diary. All thanks to you and God. Wondering why you? In fact, today I'm still alive because of you. Without you, I would not have anyone to share my pains with, and I don't think that I would have survived all the pains. Thank you.

I know he wants a shoulder to cry. I know how much it hurts when someone you love is in love with someone else. I have experienced it till now, and he is experiencing it now. I shared it with you, and he will share it with me. Just the way I love you, he will also start loving me. I hope at least now my new life begins. I hope God would let me smile at least from now on. Goodnight, Diary.

19 May 1986

Wondering why I'm so late to come to you? It's because I had hell to attend. Just now, I came from hell, and it's still painful. In fact, yesterday I had told you about the break-up. I indeed opted for a better life. But you know what happened? It has become worse. Today he was home. He was drunk. He was abusing girls. He has started to hate all women. He thinks all girls are cheats. He created a big scene. My mother-in-law just went inside her room and locked herself to sleep. I tried to bring him to the room, but he was uncontrollable. And I experienced my first sex. In fact, it was a rape on me. I'm crying in front of you and writing. He never had the love. He just rushed himself into me. He cursed Gagana. He tore my dress. Myarms are all red. He has scratched me all over. He slapped me, saying, 'Take it, Gagana. This is for cheating on me.' He thought that I was Gagana. He raped me in anger. I'm so scared. I came to the bathroom to write to you. I shouted. I begged him to let me go, but I was treated so badly. No one came to help me. At least my mother-in-law could have come, but all of them don't bother about me. All my dreams which I dreamt yesterday just remained dreams. I'm sure he will never love me. He has developed hatred towards all girls. He was telling me that he will go to different girls every day. He was slapping me and saying, 'Gagana, you wanted one more guy, right? I will have 100 more women.' This hurts, Diary. I mean the words, not the beatings from him.

Look at me. Your only friend is bleeding here in front of you. I wish I would just die here. I'm tired, Diary, and I'm so scared to go out of this bathroom. I will just sleep here. Be with me, Diary. Please help me out. Please . . .

7 December 1986

Hello, Diary. I have received a letter from Mom yesterday, but my mother-in-law gave it to me just today. You know how cheap she is? She has already read it. I hate her. She had written a letter to Mom last month, asking her why I was not conceiving. How can she write something like that? My mother is hurt to the core. This lady spoiled my life, and she was blaming me for not carrying her son's child. Her son has started to find his pleasure. He is having contacts with prostitutes. He started all these as a revenge against Gagana. But now he can't come out of it. He is living his life, forgetting that I'm also part of it. Yeah, he does remember me. You know when? It's when he comes late at night and still hungry for sex. Someday he might understand my sacrifice. Maybe someday he might love me. I know it's not wise to expect love from him after all these, but he is my husband. I still love him a lot, and yeah, I almost forgot, tomorrow I should go to the doctor. If they detect any problem in me, then divorce is for sure. I hope nothing is wrong in me. At times when I sit alone and think, I also feel that I should conceive soon. Maybe then he will start loving me. If not me, at least our child. Having a baby of my own would be such a great feeling. It's the symbol of my love towards him. It's the best gift which I can give him. And after seeing my child, he might leave all his addictions for it. It will be so cute?small eyes, small nose, the delicate skin touching me. The feel of the touch of motherly love?I want to experience it, Diary. I may get a life which truly loves me. Oh god, I'm so excited!

But let's hope for the best tomorrow. Goodnight.

8 December 1986

Hello, Diary. I know you will be bored of my tragedies in life. Every night I come to you with something which is always bad, but you are the only one I have to share with. Today also I have a bad news. The last hope for getting love from him has vanished. The doctor told me that I can never get pregnant with his child. And the worst part is that the defect is in him, not me. The doctor explained that his sperm count is less, and he can't get any woman pregnant. There goes the end of my dreams.

Now the whole world will humiliate him. Everyone would call him names which would hurt him. He is already hurt. I don't want him to be hurt more. Moreover, Dad and Mom will have regrets. I don't know whether I should tell him the truth. I don't know how to react. I just told my mother-in-law that everything is fine, and I promised to conceive soon. I'm thinking about everyone. What I did was correct, right? Should I hide this? I don't know. Goodnight.

Stage 4

This stage will tell you the cause of your mother's death. This stage is something related to you. This stage has something which was discovered only a few weeks back. This truly made me love your mother. Read on. You will discover about yourself.

19 December 1986

Hello, Diary. I'm very scared today. For the first time in my life, I'm scared to share something with you. I'm tense and in dilemma whether to tell you or not. Promise me that you will keep it a secret.

After hiding all these things about the report from him and my mother-in-law, I could not sleep properly. I wanted to tell them the truth. I couldn't let his self-respect go, so I made a point of telling him tonight and asked him what to do next. I was sleeping on my bed. As usual, I was scared, so I pretend to be asleep. Even when he opened the door and came in, I didn't open my eyes. I could hear him walking towards me. I knew that he will wake me up for sex, which I never wanted, but he just lay next to me. He smelled like he has drunk. I breathed a sigh of relief because I just escaped hell, but something which I never expected happened. His hand slowly moved on my shoulder and slid all the way on to my arm and held my hand. I experienced a different touch today. He was delicate. He was soft. In fact, for the very first time, I felt the love.

I realized that he loves me. He is showing it when I'm asleep, and he doesn't want me to know about it. Something soft just brushed on my back. I guess it was his lips. Soon I was pleasured with kisses on my back. The kisses continued from the back to the side of my hips and even went all over my abdomen. I felt something soft tickling me. I guess it was his tongue. The kiss followed on my arms and then near to my neck. I could not open my eyes, fearing that he might stop showing love. Everything he did had so much love in it. His hands slowly held my cheeks. Soon my face was in his palms. He kissed me on my forehead. My eyes started getting wet in happiness. He kissed my eyes. I hugged him tight. Soon we were inseparable. There were no words exchanged, but the touch told everything. Every time he moved his palm over my head, I understood that he doesn't want to hurt me anymore. For the first time, I was involved in lovemaking. His broad shoulders were enough to let me in them forever. I was lost in his love, and before I could realize what happened, we finished our lovemaking. We just lay down next to each other.

It was the best sex of my life. In fact, the only sex in which I involved myself. I slept on his shoulder with closed eyes. Then a voice made me open my eyes in surprise. I opened them. I could see Samuel on my bed, lying with me. I was drawn back. I instantly ran into the bathroom. I sat down in shock. The sex which I had today was with Samuel. My husband was heavily under the influence of alcohol, so Samuel had to drop him home. He came into me to fulfil his desires. All men are cheap. How could he do this to his close friend's wife? I didn't have the courage to go out and speak to him. I slept that night in the bathroom. Was this my mistake? I promise you that throughout the act I thought that it was my husband, but I was cheated. I feel so impure. I hate my own body. But trust me, I was innocent. All men use us. Being a girl is the worst thing. Diary, you trust me, right? I'm still pure from the heart. But how can I make him believe me? I'm planning to confess to him the truth tomorrow. He might think that I intentionally went to Samuel as I cannot conceive with him. How can I hide this truth? I don't know what to do, Diary. I'm crying here.

20 December 1986

Hi, Diary, I know you are eagerly waiting to know what happened today. But nothing really happened. I could not tell him. I was scared . . . Now itself he is not showing any love to me. What more if he comes to know about it? He might hate me. It's better not to be loved than to be hated. I'm thinking of forgetting about that night as if it were just a nightmare. It's just between me, you, and Samuel. Three of us will keep it as a secret. I hope the world will never know about it. I know I'm cheating on him. But if he comes to know about it, then it's not only me who will cry. People will talk about my character, and I don't want to be the pain symbol for Dad and Mom. All this is for them. Trust me; I would have died long back. Even now, I wish my very next breath is my last breath, but for my father's reputation, my mom's love, my granny's hope, and my husband's attachment, I am stopping myself. I have cried enough, Diary. I'm very sleepy. I will sleep now. Hope I get some peace, at least in the future. Goodnight.

That was how you were born! I'm not your father, Smritha. It's Samuel. The truth which she and Samuel tried to hide is now known to both of us. I know you are shocked. I know it's hard for you to digest this. Let's talk over it.

Your (so-called) dad

Same day
Time: unknown

I just can't believe what I read just now. I was literally sweating in this air-conditioned room. So the one whom I thought was my dad was actually not my father? It was Uncle Sam who was responsible for my birth. I guess that was the reason why I was being loved by him since childhood. But I couldn't digest the truth. Mother . . . my mother had gone through so much. She was such a sweet girl, and she experienced so much all through her life. She was brave. But how did she die? The questions started killing me. There were thousands of questions! But there was only one man who could answer me. I started waiting. It was a long wait. He never seemed to be coming back. My brain kept on recalling the things that happened in Kerala, and I slowly drifted away to sleep.

I felt a rough hand brushing over my cheek. I wished it was him and opened my eyes.

'Feeling better?' he said.

'I read it completely,' I replied right away. I tried to get up. He helped me to sit down on the bed, and he sat on a chair in front of me. Silence reigned for the next few minutes.

'Can you do me a favour?' I said.

'Yeah.'

'Please tell me what happened. Did you read this when she was alive and took her there to kill her? You even took Uncle Sam so that you can kill them both? Why did you leave me alive? You should have killed me there as well. Tell me what happened?' I screamed the last sentence aloud.

He smiled at me and walked towards the door.

'Please, Dad, please let me know what happened?' I cried softly. He turned back. There was happiness. He came running towards me. 'Thank you, Smritha. I'm happy that you still call me as your dad! I will tell you. It's so happened on that day when we were in Kerala that your mom and I were finally in love. It was on the beach, Smritha. Your mother was holding my hand, and we were walking along the endless sand. It seemed so beautiful. Your mother and I had totally forgotten about you! We noticed the huge waves. I began to worry a little. At that time, I had no clue about all these secrets of your mother's life. We both walked to the place where you and Samuel were relaxing. You were talking over the phone. Samuel came towards us. You were standing alone, talking on the phone full of excitement. Your mother wanted the camera which we had left in the car. She told me to shoot a photo of yours. She was so happy to see you so happy, and the sea behind you would make that picture a great frame. I left for the camera.

'Your mom and Samuel were watching the sea and began to speak. I remembered that I didn't leave the camera in the car but have carried it all along in my bag. I came running to take your picture, but their conversation made me hide myself and listen. She was telling Samuel to stop showing love to you. It might make me have doubts about the truth. She spoke out the truth, and I came to know all about this from their conversation. I realized that I'm not your genetically father. I thought your mother had cheated on me. I have hated women after I saw the nature of Gagana. I was gaining back the trust, seeing your mother. But now I went ferocious, thinking that your mother is a cheat. I could not believe that she and my best friends cheated on me. At that moment, I thought that your mother had a relationship with Samuel.

'I made myself visible to them, and my facial expression made them understood that I had realized the truth. Your mother didn't speak a word. Samuel told me it just happened once, and I slapped him. At the same time, we heard your scream. You were hit by a wave. Samuel ran to you. Your mother told me her last sentence: "Throughout my life, I have loved only one person, and that's you. I know that I have lost your love, and I can't live any more." She ran into the sea. Waves were pushing her out, but she kept on running. I'm a cruel man, Smritha, I just watched her. I didn't even call her name. Samuel came running to me, holding you. You were unconscious. He asked me about your mother. I showed him the sea. He ran to save her, but both of them didn't return.

'A few days later, I brought you back here, and I started to live my old life. I thought all women are born to cheat, so I started using different women daily. But it so happened that recently, a few weeks back, I found one of her diaries. I read many interesting things in it, and I searched your mom's room for more dairies. I found them all. I started reading them. I understood the sweetness of your mother. I realized her last words were actually the truth. I realized how much she loved me. She hid the truth that I can't get any woman pregnant to make the whole world not to humiliate me. She, in fact, did everything for my happiness. I love your mother, Smritha. I just love your mother.' He fell down from the chair, crying.

'Dad . . .' I pulled out the drip and ran to him.

'You still accept me as your dad?' He looked right into my eyes. It was red and filled with tears.

'Obviously, Dad. You realized your mistakes. Mom will be happy now.' I hugged him tightly, and we both realized the love within us for each other.

'Smritha, you won't leave me, right? Don't do anything like your mother, please. I have only you in my life. I don't have anyone else. I promise you that I will remain as your responsible father. Trust me, affection is greater than perfection.' I wiped his tears and held his hand.

Chapter 23

Six years later

I was enjoying the breeze from the window to my left. I turned right, and he turned towards me!

'Look in front and drive,' I said.

'I can see the whole world in your eyes. You think I can't see the road?' Pradeep smiled and changed the gear. I began to think about the past. Almost six years had passed. From there, I left you all with my story. Life is different now. I married my Pradeep. All thanks to my dad. He saved me from my death, and he got me married to Pradeep. Soon after, when I got out well from the hospital, results were out. I scored less, as I expected. Pradeep got into medical. Poo got into engineering. I joined to a degree. Dad's support and Mom's wishes were with me to guide me to be strong. When the whole world was commenting on my marks, Dad stood up for me. He asked me to do well in my bachelor of science degree. I did not disappoint him. Not only did I prove to the world, I also proved to myself that I can succeed. Soon after Pradeep left me, I kept myself busy with studies and my forgotten passion for music.I realized the happiness of being true. Two years back, Dad met Pradeep in a family function. Pradeep had proposed to Dad that he wanted to marry me.

He was angry for what I did, but not for what I am. We spoke regarding our past and where it went wrong. I agreed that I made a mistake by betraying him and braking down his trust but that would not define my character. I was just too immature and insecure. Pradeep was also ashamed and apologized for what he did to me. He realised that judging a girl by making them go through tests is insane. I promised him that I can be a better person for him, but I made sure that he understood that I cannot change myself for him. Attraction towards good looking opposite sex is normal. That's how nature designed us to be, but we should be strong enough to pull back ourselves against them especially when we are committed to someone else. I guess all these experiences made me stronger. I was able to judge what is correct and what is not.

Today Pradeep is one of the best doctors in town. We moved to a new house which Dad gifted me. We got this new car from Pradeep's money. It's been a year since I got married to Pradeep, and life turned out to be a happy cup of tea.

Poo got into a meaningful life. She got into one of the software companies and now working as a software engineer. She is married and living a somewhat happy life. But deep inside her, she has the pain. She has the guilt. Today she is married to one of the richest men in town, but it's not the one whom she loved. It's not one whom she wanted. She never informed her parents about the love she had towards Amar. She didn't even let him talk to her parents. I guess it was the biggest mistake which she did in her life. Her parents might have accepted him. She didn't even try. Today she regrets it and curses herself for the loss of a life.

Yes, Amar is dead. He is no more. He committed suicide on the day of her marriage. No one except Poo and me knew the reason of his death, and we made sure that their love remained secret, the secret which is killing my sensitive Poo. He was placed in a multinational company. His parents had huge dreams for him, but he left them in pain. Amar is a special character in my life. He was the one who came close to me only in my imaginations, and losing him was a huge pain to me. But for Poo, he was her reality. He had cared for her so much. He had thought about her comfort every second. I wondered how Poo balanced all this and smiled after her marriage. Recently, she burst into tears, thinking about the past. The situations were so cruel that she couldn't come to see him dead. Idiotic Amar, he simply sacrificed his life to a girl who couldn't even attend his funeral. My Poo was in between two things. On one side, she had her parent's reputation and the amount of trust they had on her, and on the other side, someone who trusted her and dedicated all these years for her happiness. She chose her parents' trust over Amar's love. I know that parents are important part of our life. They are the living gods who are responsible for what we are today, but she could have balanced the two. She didn't even tried. In my words,'She killed him.' Her parents are the ones who brought her up. It's expected and obvious that they should love her. But who is Amar? He was a stranger. He was never related to her. He was born and brought up away from her, having no clue about her, but he loved her so much without any expectations. He was not even expecting to be loved back. And I realized how lucky I am. I got another chance even after doing so many mistakes. But she didn't even give a chance for that idiot, and he didn't have a dad like mine who could make him understand life and protect him.

Now, in front of people, Poo is a happy girl who is enjoying her life, but she cries in my arms. She feels the guilt every time her husband touches her. I understand what hell a girl experiences when she has someone in her heart and someone else on bed. But it's all her own making, and she is paying for her decisions.

Dad lives alone in the same place. I was privileged to read all the dairies of mom. I'm proud of my parents now. I read their stories and decided not to repeat the mistakes they did in their life.

'Careful, dear, loosen up your seat belt. You might hurt my daughter.' Pradeep smiled at me at my huge tummy.

Smiles followed in my face. My hands slowly moved over my tummy. I can feel my son kicking me. We both have fought about this baby. I'm expecting a son, and he wants it to be a daughter. Life became meaningful after I became a pregnant. To become a mother is a godly feel. Giving birth to another life is something which every woman wishes for?new dreams, new hopes. This child will be my future. If it turns out to be a girl, then I will make sure she won't do the mistakes that Mom, Poo, and I did. I only want happiness in my child's life. With a smile on my face and a satisfaction of being born as woman, I'm ending my story here. Love, lust, and loyalty are the three very important Ls in a girl's life. The mixture of these three would define a girl's life. Love someone more than yourself, express lust only to that someone whom you love, and be loyal to the one whom you expressed love and lust. We all make mistakes in life. Give your loved ones a chance to correct their mistakes just the way Pradeep gave me. Remember my dad's words: 'Affection is greater than perfection.'

'The 26 December 2004 tsunami significantly affected the coastal regions of southern peninsular India. About 8,835 human lives were lost in the tsunami in mainland India, with 86 persons reported missing. Kerala alone lost an estimated 200 people.

May their souls rest in peace'